I0620523

"What do you know of love
that I haven't taught you?"

Maruja screamed at Ruy, her dark eyes filled with
hate.

The young bullfighter took a deep breath. Then
he said, "What you taught me is filth. You tried to
lead me around by a nose-ring. Did my father edu-
cate me to be the kind of man who could stand by
while a murder was committed? . . . I remember,
even while I was a little boy, how you gave me too
much wine, and then, with my father sick in the
next room, we coupled like animals, and that is
what you call love."

Maruja screamed his name but her anger lodged
in her throat and her voice broke. Then she lunged
at him. When Ruy struck her arms away, his
brother Paco leapt and swung, a single blow that
sent him reeling across the room. Ruy crumpled to
his knees against the wall. A second passed. Then
he stood up, looked at us, condemning us to hell,
and grabbed a barbed pair of banderillas off the
wall.

Turning, raising the hooked sticks over his head,
he walked across the room. As sure as my name is
Drum, I knew what he had in mind, and slowly
reached into my pocket for the Beretta. In a flash
Ruy swept by my line of vision, making straight
for his brother and Maruja, the deadly sticks
poised for the kill. . . .

STEPHEN MARLOWE:

THE SECOND LONGEST NIGHT
MECCA FOR MURDER
TROUBLE IS MY NAME
MURDER IS MY DISH
KILLERS ARE MY MEAT
VIOLENCE IS MY BUSINESS
TERROR IS MY TRADE
HOMICIDE IS MY NAME
DOUBLE IN TROUBLE *(with Richard S. Prather)*
DANGER IS MY LINE
DEATH IS MY COMRADE
PERIL IS MY PAY
MANHUNT IS MY MISSION

jeopardy is
my job

by stephen marlowe

WILDSIDE PRESS

Copyright © 1962 by Fawcett Publications, Inc.

chapter one

It was a nice, quiet party—the kind they throw on the last night of Carnival or when a war ends or if the human race has about twenty-four hours to live.

The one kind of party it wasn't was the kind you'd throw if you were expecting a private detective who had just flown in three thousand miles to find your missing husband.

I stood at the bottom of a long flight of stone stairs, hefted my B-4 bag, stared up through the moonlight at the big villa on the hill and said, because I didn't quite believe it, "Are you sure this is La Atalaya?"

"Sí, señor," the kid who had led the way from the town square answered. "The Watchtower. The villa of Señora Hartshorn." Her house, not his. Robbie Hartshorn already had been missing long enough for them to have him dead and buried. But if so, his widow had a peculiar idea of mourning.

Music drifted down the steep hillside. It was bullfighter music, a pasa doble searching in the night for a torero, and laughter and shouts of "Olé!" and "Quiero!" chased it down the steep stairs that were bone-white in the moonlight. I hefted the B-4 bag again and started climbing. The villa sat high on the edge of the hill like an eagle's aerie, but I had forty pounds of luggage instead of wings. There were sixty-three steps. I counted them for no particular reason as the music got louder. They brought me to a broad terrace that looked down over the whitewashed buildings of Torremolinos and the golden moon-track on the Mediterranean beyond, and I told myself—as I had told myself before and would tell myself again—I was a long way from home.

The double doors at the end of the terrace opened to disgorge a chunky woman who walked as if she'd had one or two too many but as if she knew how to handle the result. "A lady bullfighter just told me to go soak my head," she informed me and the moonlight in a husky

5

voice. "Did a lady bullfighter ever tell you to go soak your head?" The husky-voiced, chunky woman looked me over. "No, she wouldn't. Though she might. She's a real horse's ass."

"Who?" I said.

"Come on. There's only one lady bullfighter in Torre."

"You wouldn't be Mrs. Hartshorn?" I asked.

"Don't be a horse's ass," she said indignantly. "Me? *That* horse's ass?" She laughed. It sounded like the other end of a horse whinnying. "Say, are you new around here? Maybe you've got the right idea, though, coming to one of Andrea Hartshorn's parties complete with baggage."

"Is Mrs. Hartshorn inside?"

"Who cares?" the chunky woman winked broadly. "I'm Nancy Huntington, all dressed up for a party and here it is only eleven-thirty and already my husband's fried to the eyeballs. How come you popped in so late?"

"The plane from Madrid to Malaga was delayed."

"Aren't they always? Say, you mean to tell me you flew all the way down from Madrid for one of Andrea's parties? The dirty liar told me it was a spur of the moment thing. Nancy Huntington gazed down at the moon-track and eased herself closer to me. Her perfume was musky and strong enough to have been applied by a roller. "Well, better late than never," she breathed huskily. "What's your name?"

"Chester Drum," I said. "I flew all the way from Washington, but not for a party. I'm one of Mrs. Hartshorn's hired hands."

The chunky woman froze where she stood, as if a shaft of moonlight or my words had impaled her. And what I had said finished her interest in me. "Your employer is inside," she said, grand-daming me. "Horse's ass," she mumbled under her breath.

I went through the double doors to join the other descendants of Eohippus.

A tall blonde leaning on thirty-nine hard enough to change its spots to forty was crouching in the center of a room not quite the size of a bull ring and making passes with a pink silk scarf like a bullfighter with a muleta. There were maybe fifty people in that room, most of them ignoring her with the completely casual indifference you find only at a big party and only at the expatriate watering places of the world, like St. Tropez or Palma de Majorca or Torremolinos on Spain's Costa del Sol. But two or three men were sycophantically egging her on as her bare feet moved to the rhythm of the pasa doble coming from a hi-fi in the corner. The invisible bull lunged, and she pulled back and lifted her makeshift muleta, and there were a couple of half-hearted shouts of "Olé!" The blonde flashed big teeth at them, and rolled baby-blue eyes. Then she took two more steps in time to the music, hit her shins on the edge of a cocktail table and sat down hard. She blinked and tried to smile again, but tears were bright on her cheeks. She brushed long blonde hair away from her face and tried to stand up. She couldn't make it. I realized then she was dead drunk.

"All of you," she cried, "you rotten stinking bastards, drinking my liquor, laughing at me behind my goddam back, Robbie would kick you all the hell out, didn't you ever see a girl trip before?"

There were some pained looks, but some half-hearted offers of assistance too. They were half-hearted enough for me to get there first. I caught the blonde under her shoulders. "Can you make it?" I whispered against her ear. "I'm going to take you outside for some air, Mrs. Hartshorn."

"I can make it clear down to the Club Mañana, if I want to," she said. "Who are you? I don't know you."

"Drum," I said. "Governor Hartshorn cabled you I was coming, didn't he?"

"I don't like my father-in-law."

"What does that have to do with anything? He wants to find Robbie. Don't you?"

"Of course I do," she said indignantly. Her weight was still on my arms. She had made no move to get up.

"Is throwing a party like this your idea of trying to find him?"

That made her snapping mad, which was what I wanted. She got to her feet, turned on me and cried, "What the hell can I do? I don't like my father-in-law, Mr. Drum, and I don't think I'm going to like you."

"You don't have to like me. You just have to tell me how he disappeared."

"I told the Guardia. I told the Consul in Malaga. He's still missing."

"That's why I'm here."

"You're very modest."

"The Governor thinks I'm a good detective," I said modestly.

"I don't like my father-in-law."

"Three strikes and out," I said. "Let's go." She didn't move. She was a blonde who had to be challenged. "If you think you can make it."

She snorted, and turned, and walked very steadily toward the double doors. "Where the hell are they hiding that bottle of Fundador?" someone bawled at the top of his voice as we left. "Hey, Andrea, where's the—now, where the hell did Andrea go?" An old woman in a maid's uniform smilingly asked him in Spanish what he wished. She was one of four patroling that bull ring of a room.

Mrs. Huntington had deserted the terrace. I took Andrea Hartshorn's elbow and guided her down the stairs.

We were sitting at a sidewalk table in front of the Club Mañana in the center of town. On the stucco wall behind us, a poster showing a bullfighter in his suit of lights, the kind they wear in Madrid but not in Andalucia, said that there would be four afternoons devoted to los toros at the iron bull ring at Fuengirola this week.

Andrea Hartshorn stared across the wide plaza. I stared at the poster. From a bodega across the plaza came the sound of gypsy music: rhythmic clapping in an oddly disturbing tempo and a man wailing at the top of his voice to his lost love. We were drinking hot Spanish coffee, as black and as strong as a good fighting bull. "Come on," I urged, "let's hear it." When she failed to respond, I tried needling her again. "I didn't fly three thousand miles for you to clam up on me."

"*We* flew three thousand miles fifteen years ago for a few months in the sun. Robbie needed it. We've been here ever since." She smiled with just her mouth. "Robbie is a remittance man. I'm a remittance woman. We're paid a monthly stipend to keep out of the family's hair. Remittance men. The polite word is expatriate."

"Sure," I said, "that's why you don't like the Governor."

It was another needle, but the wrong one. She drank her black coffee, cocked an ear to the flamenco wail and pretended I was three thousand miles away. I looked at the poster again and asked, because I wanted to break the silence, "Where's Fuengirola?"

"Nine miles down the Malaga-Cadiz caretera toward Gibraltar." She finished her coffee and added unexpectedly, "The last time I saw Robbie he was on his way there."

"To do what?"

"I—I'd rather not say."

"Would you rather I didn't find him?"

"You seem very confident you will."

"If a private detective doesn't handle divorce cases, and I don't, a lot of his business is bound to be skiptracing. Every Missing Persons Bureau in every police force in the States is overworked and understaffed, which is one reason the District of Columbia and the Commonwealth of Virginia license guys like me. And plenty of times when a man disappears there are reasons why his family can't or don't want to call in the police. These cases usually form a pattern, Mrs. Hartshorn. A man turns up among the missing for two reasons basically: money and sex. So if you're called in and you're given the facts, you can usually see a pattern. I'm not confident, I'm hopeful. But you could disappoint me. It isn't my spouse who's missing. You haven't told me anything yet which indicates you want him found. Maybe you don't."

"That's pretty brutally frank."

"You didn't hire me. Your father-in-law did."

"I want Robbie found. We love each other. Ours is a perfect marriage."

"Congratulations. Why was he on his way to Fuengirola?"

"You don't understand. We—someone else is involved."

"Someone else is always involved. What's the pattern, Mrs. Hartshorn? Money or sex?"

"You're so smug. I hate smug men."

I wasn't smug. I was trying to establish a client-investigator relationship with her, trying to build her confidence in me even if she wound up hating me the way a patient hates his analyst in the beginning, and getting nowhere fast. "Who else is involved?"

"That's none of your business. I wish you hadn't come here." She lit a cigarette. "The Guardia will find him."

"He's been missing how long? Two weeks? You were worried enough to write the Governor about it."

"No I wasn't. Robbie always cashes his remittance check on the first of the month. When he didn't this month, the Governor wrote us. When I didn't answer, he got in touch with the Consul in Malaga. That's why you're here."

"Then you're not worried? Has Robbie up and disappeared like this before?"

"No. We're always together. Always. I'm worried. I'm frantic. But—" She let her words trail off. The gypsy clapping across the plaza seemed louder.

"But someone else is involved. Who?"

The other sidewalk tables outside the Club Mañana had begun to fill. There was talking and laughter. I recognized some of the faces I had seen at the Hartshorn villa.

"Party's breaking up," I said.

"That's the first round. They'll be back."

At the table next to ours a woman's husky whisky-voice said, quite distinctly, "I want your husband." I wasn't only smug, I was rude. I did some staring. Four people sat at the next table. One was the chunky woman I had met on the terrace: Mrs. Huntington. Next to her sat a tall man, solidly built but with narrow shoulders. He wore his gray hair in a crewcut and leaned his jowly face on a big soft hand. He had small, stubborn, close-set eyes. He looked drunk enough to be indifferent or indifferent enough to be drunk. I decided he was Mr. Huntington. Across from them and with their backs to us sat a man and a woman.

"I said, Marcia, that I want your husband," Nancy Huntington repeated.

The other woman laughed. "Well then don't let me stand in the way, dear," she said, and her accent was north-country English. "Take him."

The man whose back was turned laughed uncertainly

and asked in Spanish, "What does she wish for? Is she very drunk?"

"She pretends to be drunker than she is," the woman replied in Spanish.

"I resemble that remark," Nancy Huntington said. "But I meant what I said. I want your—"

"I said you could take him, love. Please do. You're boring me, you know. But on the other hand if he understood English better, you'd be boring him too."

Mr. Huntington frowned. Mrs. Huntington said spitefully, "I hear you got gored by a bull before you retired. In the wrong place. I hear you can't have children."

"If I could have children, love," North-country said, "and if they looked like your children, I wouldn't want any."

Mrs. Huntington had been drinking a gin-and-tonic. She raised her glass and hurled its contents in the other woman's face. Mr. Huntington got up, looking pained. Mrs. Huntington got up too. North-country rose too. She was big. She wore tapered slacks and she was built mannishly and she must have been six feet tall in her low-heeled sandals. She leaned across the small table and swatted Mrs. Huntington indelicately across the chops. Mrs. Huntington went over backwards and landed across a chair, which promptly splintered the way breakaway chairs do in the movies. The gypsies went on clapping across the plaza. There wasn't another sound.

Mr. Huntington crouched near his wife. Her eyes blinked. The left side of her face was red from hairline to jaw. "Maybe we'd better get on home," Mr. Huntington said in a dead voice.

"I'll get you, you Maltese bitch," Mrs. Huntington told the lady bullfighter. The Spanish-speaking man hadn't left his seat. "What has happened?" he asked. I realized then that he was blind.

It was over a minute after that. Mr. Huntington dropped two hundred-peseta notes on the table, helped his wife to her feet and walked off into the darkness with her. The lady bullfighter told Andrea Hartshorn, "It started at your party, you know."

"I know, Marcia. I saw."

"Fernando wouldn't spit on the best part of her. But then, she really oughtn't to have hurled her drink at me."

Then the blind man got up. He looked about forty-five with long dark hair going gray, a handsome broad-cheekboned face, and shoulders like a weight-lifter's. His eyes had the blank stare of the blind.

"Me gusté la fiesta," he told Andrea Hartshorn.

"Me alegro mucho," she said automatically. I'm very glad. Then the blind man and his bullfighter wife left, his hand on her forearm. I heard the buzz of conversation at the tables around us again.

"I like your friends," I told Mrs. Hartshorn.

"Marcia and Fernando are nice. She was born on Malta, her parents were Yorkshire and she used to be a bullfighter at the local férias like the one in Fuengirola. She was gored, and that ended it. Fernando is a local product. He was an artist, and not at all bad. He went away for a year—let me see—about three years ago, and came back to Torremolinos blind. No one knows how. He isn't talking. He turned to sculpture, and he makes a pretty good living at that too. Marcia married him two years ago."

"No. I meant the other ones."

"They claim to be independently wealthy. Huntington's an old New England name, and they claim a blood-line clean back to the Mayflower. Talk is he's really on a government pension. But they do manage to live well. Half the time she's as snooty as a duchess and the other half she chases anything in pants. Not that Fernando isn't attractive." Liquor or the scene we had witnessed finally had loosened Andrea Hartshorn's tongue. "Lots of women are attracted to that combination of virility and helplessness. Anyhow, Stu Huntington wears the biggest pair of horns in Torremolinos, and they grow them pretty big around here as you may have guessed. There's talk he gets his kicks that way and is a stallion in bed after one of Nancy's sordid little escapades. Or am I shocking you?"

"I'll never be the same," I said. "Aren't there any secrets around here?" I answered my own question, "Yeah, there's one. Why, how, and where your husband vanished."

"Maybe now you can see why I don't want to talk."

"Then that's your mistake. If a private eye didn't respect his clients' confidence, he wouldn't be in business very long."

Mrs. Hartshorn looked at me. "I can use a drink. Fundador. A double."

I ordered two of them. She put hers back in one enormous gulp while I savored mine and watched the expression change on her face. Fundador was Spanish brandy, mellow and smooth. The blonde's expression changed from worried to doubtful to certain in as much time as it took me to finish my drink.

"The other person involved," she said, "is Tenley."

"That's the Governor's granddaughter, right?"

"I wish you hadn't put it that way. Tenley's *my* daughter, after all."

She was right, of course. I said, "The Governor's always talking about her. He sent her to school in Switzerland, didn't he?"

"Geneva, yes. He dotes on Tenley because he's disappointed in Robbie. But he's worried too, because he thinks she's wild."

"What do you think?"

"I think she's full of life. I also think Switzerland was a mistake. I can raise my own daughter," Mrs. Hartshorn said angrily. "She wasn't wild until—until after that finishing school in Geneva. Kids from broken marriages go there. So what if they're rich? But Robbie and me—"

I didn't want her going maudlin on me, now that she was talking. I said, "How is she involved?"

"There's a bullfighter. Not a torero, really, because he was trampled once and his leg was broken and now he can't work close to the bull. But he's really terrific with banderillas. His name is Ruy Fuentes. Robbie thought Tenley was having an affair with him."

"What do you think?"

"Tenley's a good girl," she said frostily. "Fuentes lives in Fuengirola. He's quite young, only twenty-one or -two. Two weeks ago Robbie took the bus to Fuengirola to talk to him."

"Just talk to him?"

"Well, thrash him maybe. Robbie could do it. He's got a temper, and he's strong. He never got there. Or if he got there, Fuentes lied and said he never got there. And that's it, Mr. Drum."

"Where's Tenley now?"

"In Fuengirola for the féria. Bullfighting is one of her two passions. The other one is skiing. She learned that in Switzerland."

"She's there by herself?"

"Is that some kind of an insinuation?" Mrs. Hartshorn said hotly.

"Just a question."

"Then yes. By herself because she can take care of herself."

"You tell the Guardia about Fuentes?"

"How could I? Tenley's only nineteen. It would be all over Torre before I could blink my eyes."

"Some Guardia," I said.

"They trade information for information. Real-estate men, hotel conserjes, bodega proprietors, members of the dear old fraternity of remittance men who don't like the way you mix a martini—everyone and everyone's best friend can be an informer in Spain. That's something you come to accept. Will you go to Fuengirola?"

Money or sex. In a disappearance there's usually a pattern. This time it looked like sex—with nineteen-year-old Tenley Hartshorn up to her bullfighting passion in it.

I nodded. "And thanks for your trust."

Then her face crumpled. "Find Robbie. Find him. I love him. I've been so frantic."

chapter two

It takes an expert to tell the work of a superb matador from the work of a merely adequate one who knows his limitations and is in there to punch his time clock and collect his pesetas, but you don't have to be an afficionado with a seat in the sun and a Hemingway beard and a wineskin slung over your shoulder to separate the men from the boys when it comes to the dangerous skill of charging at a tangent into the path of a galloping bull and planting a pair of barbed spikes called banderillas in the ridge of muscle behind its huge head.

Ruy Fuentes was a banderillero. I first saw him plying his deadly trade the next afternoon in the bull ring at

Fuengirola. His job, like that of the picador who sat astride a padded and blindfolded nag and wore armor from the waist down, was to weaken the bull, and particularly the ridge of muscle on the bull's neck, for the sword of the matador. Ruy Fuentes wore an Andalucian costume—dark gray suit with cutaway jacket, frilly shirt and narrow-legged trousers, cowboy boots and a broad-brimmed, flat-crowned black hat.

Four times that hot June afternoon I saw him work. He would stand across the ring from twelve-hundred pounds of enraged bull, shout, beckon imperiously and sprint across the sand with a ribboned banderilla held in each hand as daintily as a fairy holds her wand. The bull would snort, and paw, and gallop to meet him, head down, curving horns gleaming in the sunlight. There was a point in the ring where animal and slim gray figure seemed destined to meet. Then Fuentes' arms went up and the bull's head went even lower, and then for an instant they hung together, the bull ready to toss its head and gore with those savage horns, the man ready to plant his banderillas. If he did it right, and each time Fuentes did it exactly right, there was a split-second when Fuentes hung poised, high on his toes, arms up-stretched, between the bull's horns. Then his arms blurred down, the bull bellowed, Fuentes ran clear and the two banderillas, their ribbons fluttering, their barbed hooks trickling blood, hung an inch apart in the center of the ridge of muscle on the bull's neck.

There were four matadors and four fighting bulls to dispose of. Two of the matadors were proficient and two were butchers, and Ruy Fuentes, a contemptuous look on his grave, handsome face because he knew the glory belonged to the matadors and he would win no ears or tail or zapata for his work, stole the show. Each time he came out the crowd would sigh to silence as he rushed headlong to meet his destiny between the bull's horns, and each time they would respond to his work with shouts of "Olé!" and even "Torero!" though young Ruy Fuentes' bullfighting days already were behind him. He never acknowledged the acclaim with so much as a bow. He just stalked off, a solitary figure in the sun, as the trumpet sounded for the matador.

At twenty-two he was a has-been, a torero who'd been

trampled and had to settle for a secondary role in the fiesta brava. But at twenty-two he had more pride and dignity than you'd expect under those or any circumstances. I found myself hoping he wouldn't be involved in Robbie Hartshorn's disappearance even though that would mean my one and only lead had petered out.

Long late-afternoon shadows were dark under the iron-pipe and wooden slat scaffolding of Fuengirola's makeshift bull ring when I went below the grandstand and watched a yellow jeep haul the carcass of the final bull out with two urchins dressed in rags riding proudly on its bloody flank and trying to remove the banderillas. A knot of people had gathered around the four matadors whose teeth gleamed in wide smiles. Aficionados mirrored those smiles. They said a word or two, they laughed nervously, their hands reached out to touch the matadors, their heads nodded like corks bobbing on water whenever the matadors deigned to answer them.

Ruy Fuentes stood off to one side, alone with the picador. He kneeled and helped the horseman remove his greaves. When he straightened up next to the picador, at first I thought Fuentes was unexpectedly small. The picador towered over him. He looked ten years older than Fuentes. His face was long and horse-like and his wide-spaced eyes smouldered with anger and resentment, possibly because of all the men involved in the drama of the bull ring only the picador sitting high on his horse in his armor and with his heavy, eight-foot lance is hated.

I heard him say, "Those cabrons, those goats, all the world flocks to them and would kiss their rears while it is you who has made the fiesta brava a success."

"It is not their fault I was trampled, Paco," Ruy Fuentes said in a soft, deep voice, and he managed to say that not with self-pity but with a quiet dignity that matched his bearing and his face. His black hair was shorter than a Spaniard usually wears it, almost a brush-cut. His skin was dark, his nose high-bridged and proud. His black eyes just missed being arrogant, his jaw was almost as long as the picador's but his lips were soft and red, like a woman's.

Then, as I reached them, I realized he was no shrimp. I'm six-one, but the picador dwarfed me. Before hang-

ing out my private eye shingle and before my stint with
the FBI, I played running guard for William and Mary
College and even made All-State, but if he could move
I'd have hated having a guy the size of the picador Paco
playing across the line from me. He was really big,
and he looked as easy to knock down as a cross-country
moving van.

"Señor Fuentes?" I said.

When Paco looked surprised and Ruy Fuentes nodded
curtly, I asked, "Do you speak English? I don't have
any Spanish and I'd like to talk to you." The first part
of that was a lie; my Spanish is pretty good because I've
knocked around some in Latin America. But working
a case in a foreign country, where your P.I. license
wouldn't buy you a loaf of bread if you were starving,
you have very few advantages. One of them is pretended
ignorance of the language.

He answered my question by saying in English, "What
do you wish of me?"

Paco surprised me by having English too. He used it
to say, jerking a big thumb in the direction of the matadors, "You have made a mistake. You don't want Ruy
Fuentes. He is only a banderillero. Over there are the
toreros."

"I've seen better toreros in Venezuela," I said, "where
they're just beginning to learn which end of the bull is
which."

Paco smiled, but Ruy Fuentes still seemed polite but
indifferent. The big picador asked, "You have afición
then? You love the fiesta brava? You understand it?"

"No," I admitted truthfully. "But I recognize a good
banderillero when I see one."

"Thank you," Ruy Fuentes said gravely.

It was a start, and it was the truth, but I didn't like
myself for it. You can get what you want by being ingra-
tiating, just as you can get what you want by using a pair
of brass knucks. Neither way was my idea on how to
operate, and though Fuentes deserved the compliment
and I meant it, I was annoyed with myself—enough to
say, "Does Tenley Hartshorn?"

"Does Señorita Hartshorn what?" Ruy Fuentes demanded, and a chunk of dry ice wouldn't have steamed
on his tongue.

"Recognize a good banderillero when she sees one."

The picador lifted his greaves and tucked them under his arm. They looked like a toy knight's toy leg-armor there. Ruy Fuentes said, "Who are you, señor?"

"The name is Drum. I was hired by Governor Hartshorn in Maryland to find his son. Two weeks ago Robbie Hartshorn took the bus from Torremolinos to Fuengirola. He hasn't been seen since."

"Why come to us, hombre?" Paco said in a tight, menacing voice. "Many people ride the bus to Fuengirola."

In Spanish Ruy Fuentes said quickly, "I'll attend to this, Paco." He told me, "I saw Señor Hartshorn some time ago, yes. It may have been two weeks ago, as you suggest. You say he is missing?"

I said he was missing. "What did you see him about?"

"A personal matter."

"He came here to tell you to keep away from his daughter, didn't he?"

"No one tells me whom to—"

"I'm not making a moral issue out of it. I'm looking for facts—and Robbie Hartshorn. Did you fight?"

"He is a middle-aged man," Ruy Fuentes said.

"He's forty-two and from what I hear as strong as an ox. You'd have to be pretty good to take him."

Paco rumbled, "You have no right to question us."

"I'm not questioning you," I said. "I wouldn't know you from any other big stiff who rides a horse and sticks a stopped lance in a bull's back. I'm talking to Señor Fuentes."

"He is my brother," Paco said, more tightly. He hadn't liked my dig at his unappreciated line of work, but I hadn't liked the menace sprouting like a weed in his voice.

"I wouldn't fight with Señor Hartshorn," Ruy Fuentes told me. "All the time he is muy borracho—very drunk. We argued, yes. He left still angry. Tenley is a woman. No man, not even her father or perhaps least of all her father, can guide her steps. We are in love."

"That's all that happened? An argument?"

"Yes, I have told you. And then he left."

"Where's Tenley Hartshorn now?"

As if in answer to my question, a girl's voice called, "Ruy! Oh Ruy, you were magnificent!"

I didn't watch her approach, but looked at Ruy Fuentes' face instead. It was as if the soft, sensitive, girlish mouth had taken over from the proud masculine eyes, nose and jaw. Ruy Fuentes looked suddenly shy. He held his hat in front of him and fingered the broad brim nervously. He shifted his weight from one foot to the other and smiled like a sub-deb greeting her first date. Then he walked past me. As far as it mattered to him, I was no longer there.

And then I saw why. A girl, and from the look on Ruy Fuentes' face she had to be Tenley Hartshorn, was crouching at the end of one of the grandstand benches on a level with my shoulders. She reached her hands out, but he caught her above the hips with his own hands and gently lowered her to the sand. She smiled at him as if he had performed an act of gallantry meriting knighthood. He smiled at her as if his world was complete for the first time today.

I didn't blame him. Even the aficionados still jabbering away at the toreros stopped to stare. She was a tall and slender sun-tanned brunette in a simple summery dress the green color of the Mediterranean under a bright sunlit sky—which is like saying Dominguén kills cattle for a living. She moved lithely and unself-consciously, like a cat. Her eyes were the same green as her dress and their whites were very white against the tan of her face. The rest of her features were nice enough, but nothing to make an aficionado forget what had brought him to the iron bull ring in Fuengirola. Still, there was something intangible about her that really got you. She was beautiful the way a painting you don't quite understand can be beautiful. Maybe it was those eyes. Maybe it was the way her high and wide-spaced cheekbones made those big green eyes seem even bigger, or the way they drew her tanned skin taut, or the way they shadowed her cheeks and accentuated the ripe red surprise of her lips. Or maybe I was staring too much, because Tenley Hartshorn's radiant smile changed to a wry one, and the wry smile was one she had used before and for the same reason, a wry acceptance of the fact that men will be men, and Ruy Fuentes cleared his throat and said, "Tenley, this is Mr. Drum. He says he is looking for your father."

"What for?" Tenley Hartshorn said, not smiling.

"He's been missing two weeks. The Governor was worried."

"He'll come home when he runs out of money. He always does, after one of his benders."

"You think he's on a bender?"

"If you knew my father," Tenley Hartshorn said sullenly, "you wouldn't have to ask that question. He's gone off on them often enough when my mother can't keep up with his drinking. Not that she doesn't try," Tenley added spitefully.

"Admire them both, do you?" I said.

"Is that supposed to be funny?"

"If you think it's funny. The Hartshorn women, mother and daughter, throw me. You mother wouldn't cooperate at first because she didn't want to drag you into this. You're convinced your old man's on a harmless bender even though the Governor was worried enough to send a detective three thousand miles to find him."

"I'll start worrying when I think there's something to worry about."

"Your grandfather does."

"He hasn't spent his life with them, and neither have you. But I have. Starting before breakfast they drink themselves into a stupor all day—until it's time to brush their teeth with Fundador before going to bed." I must have given her a funny look, because she went right on, "And if you think I have no right telling this to a stranger, it's no secret. It's something the whole Costa del Sol knows—when the whole Costa del Sol isn't doing likewise. Have you been here long enough, Mr. Drum, to see the pathetic little feral-eyed and dirty-faced children slinking around all the patios on all the villas on the hills over Torremolinos? They can't speak English and the Spanish they learn from the servants is gutter Spanish, and maybe if they're lucky they can read and write by the time they're nine or ten. Their parents are too drunk to care about them, you see. When you're an alcoholic expatriate in Spain, mañana isn't just a word, it's a way of life. I was one of those kids until the Governor sent me off to school in Switzerland. If he hadn't, the monthly checks would have stopped coming, so Andrea and Robbie gave him the green light. Come to think of it, they were probably glad to be rid of me for a few years."

That was quite a speech. It left her with a flush under the tan of her cheeks, and her green eyes looked two shades darker.

"Why'd you bother coming back from Switzerland?" I asked.

She looked at Ruy Fuentes, and the way she looked at him was answer enough, but she told me, "Because I feel sorry for them. I guess pity's the worst emotion you can feel for someone you love, but that's the way I feel." Her almost pulverizing beauty and her indictment of the expatriate set made me forget she was just a kid, but when she spoke of her own feelings with a teen-ager's grave and somehow weary self-assurance, I remembered she was only nineteen. I forgot it again when she displayed a bear-trap brain by asking, "Andrea didn't want to drag me into what?"

When I told her, she turned angrily to Ruy Fuentes. "You never said my father came to see you."

"It would only have upset you, Tenley."

"How Spanish can you get? I'm not in a cloister. I'm living the only life I'll ever live. Let me decide what's going to upset me and what isn't, will you?"

"I am Spanish," Ruy Fuentes said gravely.

She glared at him, and then the glare became a grin, and then the grin faded and the way she looked after that was very much in love. "Sure," she said. "You *are* Spanish. Maybe that's why I love you. Take care of me, Ruy. Take care of me always."

If the look that passed between them meant anything, that would be easy. Then Ruy Fuentes told her to wait outside.

"Does that come under the heading of taking care of me?"

Ruy Fuentes said that it did.

"All right, but first I want to ask Mr. Drum something. Are you going to keep on looking for him? You'll be wasting your time. He'll come home. But the Governor's got lots of money, hasn't he, and you earned a free trip to Spain as well. I can see I'm really going to like you."

"Like mother like daughter," I said, though of course she wouldn't understand. Instead of trying to, she walked out under the grandstand and through the gate where the bull truck had been backed earlier.

There was a silence which Paco broke by asking his brother in Spanish, "Does the little one know?"

"No. How could she? You heard her say it. There is no need to worry. She did not know her father was at the cueva." At first I didn't know what the word cueva meant, but then it came to me. In Spanish cueva is cave.

"Seguro?" Paco asked doubtfully.

"Claro, mi hermano. You have no need to worry." To me Ruy Fuentes said in English, "She is a very high-strung girl, my novia. You have upset her. I think it would be better if you flew home to America. Here you have no authority."

"I've been paid to do a job."

"And I have Tenley's feelings to consider. I have warned you, señor."

He went out after Tenley, leaving his big gun behind. His big gun told me, "If you upset Señorita Hartshorn, you upset my brother as well. Three more days he must stick the bulls, señor. He must be calm, and of a single purpose. Go back where you came from, or go back to Torremolinos. That is where Señor Hartshorn lives, and where you should look for him. My brother must remain calm. I would not wish him to have an accident."

It was reasonable enough up to that point, but when I didn't answer Paco said, "That is this time. This time it is words. But the next time I will not use words."

I watched him leave, all two-hundred and fifty pounds of him. A gorgeous dish who was contemptuous of her parents and called it pity, a couple of English-speaking bullfighters, a threat as thinly veiled as a belly-dancer's navel, I thought, mulling it all over, and not a clue as to the whereabouts of Robbie Hartshorn. Unless the cave that had Paco all hot and bothered was a clue.

I decided to find the cave.

chapter three

The only kind of secrets you can keep in a small Spanish town are the kind you take to the grave.

By the time it got dark, which was an hour after I

left the iron bull ring, and by dint of visiting two bodegas and drinking white wine and eating grilled sardines
fresh from the sea and heaps of clams no bigger than
my thumbnail, I knew most of what there was to know
about the Fuentes brothers and their cave. Most, not
all. That is the trouble with a town that seems to hold no
secrets. It is the one it does hold, or has no knowledge
about, that can get you killed.

In the first bodega, an old monosabio—or wise monkey—who had dreams of wearing a suit of lights in Madrid and wound up raking the sand in the provincial bull
rings and opening the gate and scurrying behind the barrier when the bull came thundering out, told me, "The
cave of Fuentes? But of course, señor. All the world in
Fuengirola knows the cave of Fuentes. One walks up the
caretera three kilometers in the direction of Torremolinos. Then one takes the dirt track into the hills perhaps
a kilometer more, and there on the left where a cactus as big as a house grows, one sees a burro-trail. Half
a kilometer along the burro-trail, and one reaches the
cave of Fuentes."

"The brothers own it?" I said. "What do they do there?"

"They live there, señor."

"Live there?"

"Claro. It is as I have said."

In the second bodega, the barman told me, "Sí, señor.
It is as you have heard. The brothers Fuentes live in a
cave not four kilometers from Fuengirola."

"I thought only gypsies—"

"Gitanos? Sí, but others as well. There is a feeling of
the heart here in my land that it is the things of civili-
zation which have brought hardship and poverty to
Spain. There was a time, señor, when the rest of Europe
did not say Africa begins at the Pyrenees, but they say
it now. Many feel this is because we try to copy the
ways of Francia and Inglaterra. But living in a cave—
oh, yes, that is very Spanish."

The barman drew another wine from the cask for me.
"The father of the Fuentes brothers, who was of an old
noble family and a poet as well, but as poor as any gypsy
—he died three years ago, señor—had a dream. We would
return to caves, he said, we would leave the foolishness of
big cars and telephones and ugly structures of steel and

glass behind us, and we would think pure thoughts and our land would return to its time of greatness, when the conquistadores explored *your* land. Don Antonio, for that was his name, wished to gather a cave village of other poets and artists and men who make music, and live with them the simple life.

"But fate struck him down early, a thing of the lungs, señor, and there was just the one cave. Don Antonio raised his sons there, and as his wife was dead he took a gypsy woman to live with him. Her name is Maruja, and it is a joke for all the world to call her Doña Maruja, especially as—now that Don Antonio is dead—his ghost must haunt that cave. For electric lights have been strung, it has been quarried out to make many rooms, there are carpets from Morocco on the floor and running water and a telephone and a phonograph that blares music into the night, frightening the burros on the mountain, and furniture has been brought in to make the caves of Fuentes a very palace. . . . More wine, señor?"

"And one for you as well."

"Don Antonio always believed that if we would fight the ways of all that Francia to the north and of Inglaterra on its island in the sea, we must first understand them. So he took upon himself the education of his boys, and as he was a great scholar himself, he taught them French and English also. But still, they were strange wild boys, as in their youth they rarely saw anyone but Don Antonio and the gypsy woman Maruja. And all the world says when they decided on the fiesta brava as a way of life, that was what killed Don Antonio, not the thing of the lungs. But Maruja was pleased, as the fiesta brava meant money. She is still young, Maruja; she was only fifteen when Don Antonio brought her to the cave ten, perhaps eleven years ago. She cried when Ruy Fuentes was trampled by a bull the same year his father died, some say more for the son than the father. Since then she has been seen no more in Fuengirola, though because she sings in the night one still knows she lives in the cave of Fuentes. And, amigo, all the world laughs behind the back of an American woman, the tall dark one who truly has afición, for though she loves Ruy Fuentes, it is clear that if the gitana Maruja so much as crooks her little finger, Ruy will come running—and not as a son to his foster-mother. But then, the gypsies have strange powers. . . . Another vino blanco, señor?"

How much of what he had said was truth and how much could be explained by the fact that the Spanish are the most voluble people in the world, I didn't know. When he began to talk of a flamenco dancer who would perform at the bodega later, I asked for my check and paid it after he toted it up in chalk on the surface of the bar.

As I was leaving, Stu Huntington and the blind sculptor Fernando entered the bodega. After the fun and games between their wives last night, I was surprised to see them together. But though the blind man's face was impassive and his hand rested on Huntington's forearm out of necessity, his companion's eyes were stony, his face was red to the hairline of his gray crewcut and his jowls were quivering with anger. They passed me, and there was no flicker of recognition in Huntington's eyes. I lingered in the batwing doorway. They sat at a table and leaned across it and argued in low tones. The tables on either side were occupied. Eavesdropping is as much a part of a detective's work as planting his elbows on a bar and listening to a barman who talks a blue streak, but there was no way I could do it here without being obvious. I shrugged and went out.

After I turned left at a prickly-pear cactus that *was* as big as a house, the burro-trail climbed steeply. On my right the foothills of the Sierra Tecada Mountains rose black against the moonlight. I smelled the smoke of cooking-fires and on the step-like tiers of the hillside saw the red fire-glow at the entrances to gypsy caves. On my left the hill dropped away sharply; far off I could see the white cluster of buildings that was Fuengirola in the moonlight, and the dappled reflection of the moon on the Mediterranean. In one of the caves someone was plucking a guitar and singing. The melody had Africa and the Levant in it, and a thousand years of gypsy wandering. It sang with a strange affectionate sadness of hunger and hardship and death.

The burro-trail was wider than I had expected, ten feet across, but unpaved and seamed with the twisting, dry beds of streams that already had run out of water by late spring. Along with the mournful gypsy music they reminded me that Spain was a harsh, hard land where only the very rich among men, or the dishonest, and only the carrion-eaters among animals, ate well.

I began to wonder how I would tell the cave of Fuentes from the others dotting the hillside when I heard a car behind me. I got off the road and crouched against the flank of the hill, waiting. The car roared closer, the sound of its engine as incongruous on that burro-trail as a Spanish accent at a meeting of the D.A.R. Then I saw it, a low-slung sports job pursued up the steep trail by its own cloud of dust. There had been a sports car just like it, a sleek Lancia that would clip you for eight or ten thousand bucks, parked outside the second bodega in Fuengirola. The top was down then and it was down now. In the moonlight as it sped by I saw Stu Huntington behind the wheel and blind Fernando beside him. I decided for no reason at all that they would lead me where the Fuentes brothers lived. Then I was choking in their dust, and then I started walking again.

It wasn't far, but they had two-hundred horsepower and I had shank's mare. By the time I reached the car, it was parked and empty. But the engine was still ticking under the long hood, like an expensive watch.

The burro-trail ended there. Ahead loomed a rocky slope that even a mountain goat would have shunned. At the end of the trail gaped a small cave entrance, and ten yards below it a much larger one. A burro brayed nearby, its startlingly loud *hee-haw* resounding in the mountains.

Big cave or small? Chester Drum, spelunker, scowled, and rubbed his nose, and scratched his head, and listened to the unseen burro bray again, and said, "Don't give me the horse-laugh, brother,"—and heard a motor grind, cough and kick over with a roar. Not the Lancia; it was bigger, and the sound came from inside the large cave.

I poked my nose in there. I took three steps and heard the rattling idle of the truck's engine smooth to a loud purr as an expert hand adjusted the choke. I took three more steps and headlights sprang blindingly on in front of me. The easy idle became a roar. The truck began to move. Fear slid down my spine like a pellet of ice when I thought the truck might be wide enough to fill the width of the cave. Then I bared my teeth in something like a smile. By hugging the left wall of the cave, I'd have room to spare. It was just as well: who'd hire a long, flat private detective?

The truck rumbled by. I breathed its fumes and saw a high cab and a six-wheeled truck-bed, canvas-covered. I watched its taillights recede. If the driver hadn't seen me in his headlights, I decided, he'd be too nearsighted to tool a big rig down the mountain trail. Which meant he had seen me, and that meant whatever he was doing here was not the sort of thing to make him stand on his brakes and leap out of the truck with a tire iron in his hand by way of greeting an unexpected snooper.

That was what I thought. But then I heard a sound behind me, as of a shoe dislodging loose rock, and I had time to pivot halfway around before the roof of the cave slammed down like a punch-press, fragmenting the night and my incorrect deduction.

chapter four

Sterling Moss would have envied me.

They had installed night-lights at the speedway in Indianapolis, and all the lights had coalesced to look like a big fat full moon, and there I was sitting in the bucket-seat of my Lancia so far ahead of the pack that another car wasn't even in sight. Not only that, but look ma, no hands.

Maybe I wasn't driving though. It was a two-man racer, and a big figure sat hunched over the wheel to my left. That put me in what they call in the trade the suicide seat. The wind of our slipstream rushed by. We were really zooming along. Suicide seat? Ha-ha, that was a good one. My partner was hunched over the wheel as if his life depended on it, and his hands were glued at ten and four o'clock. He was a driver who knew his business. He wouldn't wrap us around a tree.

But he might wrap us around a rambling, spreading, thick- and twisted-limbed cactus as big as a house. Now, who had said the prickly-pear was as big as a house? Didn't remember, didn't know what that damn thing was doing here, but: "Swing around it, you sap,"

I said, and my voice sounded like a laryngitic cat mewling in an echo chamber. "You'll pile us up."

The cactus got bigger, as cacti will if you are approaching them at something like forty miles an hour. I nudged my partner with an elbow. His right hand slid off the steering wheel and hung limply between us.

"Hey!" I said, and leaned over to turn the wheel hard left myself. My driver's other hand left the wheel and he slipped sideways toward me. We missed the cactus and went bucketing along. My head began to ache suddenly as I came out of my racing-car dream of glory. The driver was leaning against me, a dead weight. I tugged at his hair to get a look at his face. His hair was short-cropped and sticky—sticky with blood. His face was Stu Huntington's except for a large dent high up on the right side where his temple had been. He looked as if he had been kicked in the head by a horse. Like most people who have been kicked in the head by a horse, he was dead.

Then I snapped out of it. I was sitting in a car, Stu Huntington's Lancia, with a dead man, Stu Huntington, behind the wheel. We were not supposed to get very far. It was a miracle we had got this far. The road was more than a dirt track, but no superhighway. The grade was steep now, ten degrees going down. No shoulder bordered the left side of the unpaved road. It skirted the edge of a cliff and it was a long way down, almost vertical, to the Torremolinos-Fuengirola highway. Beyond that, the sea. Where, after going off the road and smashing flat on the highway, we were supposed to wind up.

I leaned over the dead man and gripped the wheel. My hands were shaking. His head fell in my lap. His leg was in the way. I couldn't find the brake pedal.

Our headlights swept the cliff edge. I yanked the wheel hard. We swerved and skidded, tires whining, rocks clattering under the fenders. I tromped my foot in the direction of the brake-pedal. Same no luck: his leg was still in the way. I had no room to maneuver. He held down a bucket-seat and I held down a bucket-seat, we were a big corpse and a big man, and that was that. It wouldn't help to cut the ignition. Rolling free we'd probably pick up speed even faster than in high gear. If I could reach the brake, or even the clutch-pedal to brake us down through the lower gears. . . .

I couldn't reach that either. Try getting around a dead man in the front seat of a little sports car some time.

The Lancia had a floor shift. It was low and to the right, in fourth gear. I got a grip on it. Then I had to turn the wheel to avoid the cliff edge again, and the dead man leaned against me harder. I caught a glimpse of the speedometer. It was pushing fifty—far too fast for this road, even with a racing driver behind the wheel. We had no kind of a driver at all. I grabbed the stick again and pushed hard toward the dashboard. The stick vibrated in my hand and there was a whining, grinding, scraping sound. It would be hell on the gear box, but I could worry about that later—if there was a later.

As the lower gear took hold, I felt the Lancia lurch. The speedometer needle jiggled down to forty and hovered there. I worked the gearbox down to second the same way. The Lancia bucked as if it had hit a wall, but that cut our speed to thirty and then to twenty-five. Those four-speed racers are geared to lose speed downhill in second. Maybe we'd make it. Far ahead and below us I thought I could see the white ribbon of the highway bathed in moonlight. The dirt road was fairly straight the rest of the way, though steep, but in second gear on the highway with nobody's foot on the gas we'd quickly come to a stop.

And then we blew a tire.

It was inevitable, the way the rubber had been punished running over sharp rocks in the beds of dried out freshets on the road. I clung to the wheel. It bucked and squirmed under my hands like a living thing, and I had to contend with Stu Huntington's dead weight sitting where I should have been sitting. The Lancia fishtailed in a wide slewing loop like a skier executing a Christie stop. Headlights to cliff edge again, not a very high cliff now, but more than high enough for the purpose.

The car tilted. I could see nothing. Dust enveloped us blindingly. For an awful moment I wondered if, after all, Huntington was still alive. Because I knew I had to leave the Lancia in a hurry. But no: he had to be dead. The dent in the side of his head was as big as my fist, and deep.

I fumbled with the door handle on my side and yanked it open. The car began to nose down as its front wheels left the road, it was that close. I leaped as far as I could. I didn't want to get clipped by the rear fender.

Feet-first I hit the ground, staggered two steps on a wildly bouncing treadmill, lost my balance and went down. Then I was out of the cloud of dust and rolling, and then I heard a crashing, splintering sound, and then I saw the moonlit sky and the earth, the sky again and the earth again, and the earth slammed the breath out of my lungs and the sky wouldn't give it back to me, and I was pulled and pushed and jumped on and pummeled and my mouth filled with dust, sand and pebbles.

I came to rest against a rock. I sat there, trying very hard to breathe and learning how difficult it can be. After a long time I got up. I was quaking like a leaf in a gale, but my legs held me up. I staggered in a little circle, and then a bigger one, until I found the direction I wanted, which was downhill. I made it to the bottom of the road, where it joined the highway. A short way up the pavement toward Torremolinos, a man straddling a motorbike with his feet on the ground was staring down at something. I went over there, not on the double.

The Lancia had left one fender and one wheel on the highway. What was left of Stu Huntington had been thrown clear, and it was what riveted the man on the motorbike's attention. The rest of the car had plowed through the flimsy guardrail and over some rocks into the sea.

The man on the motorbike stared and stared. When I reached him I swayed and touched him, and still looking at what lay in the road he said, very softly, "Mother of God," and was quickly and rackingly sick.

chapter five

They were really in a hurry that night—for Spain.

An hour after we had gone over, the Guardia sent a creaky old man along the road from Fuengirola on a bike. He wobbled to a stop, saw what was to be seen, solemnly removed his winged black-patent-leather hat, stood with head bowed, remounted his bike and asked me, "You wish a doctor?"

"I don't know," I said. I added on a slightly belligerent note, "This man was murdered."

"Yes," the creaky old man said in his creaky old man's voice, "clearly it was a terrible accident."

I stared at him. My Spanish is not that bad. He shrugged and began pedaling back toward town as fast as a kid who had spent the day on his bike doing nothing, enjoying every minute of it and in no hurry to get home.

My head ached and there was going to be a nasty bruise all up and down one side of my rib cage. I could feel it every time I moved my left arm. I stared out at the water, wished I hadn't finished my pack of cigarettes, and waited.

The next one to make his appearance was a cocky-looking boy in an old four-door Seat that lacked any sort of markings except a couple of fender dents. The boy got out, gave me a confident but not friendly smile and went to work shooting pictures from various angles with an archaic press camera that must have been an heirloom from the time of Primo de Rivera and a strobe light that looked brand-new.

Finally taking off his patent-leather hat the boy asked me, "He was a Catholic?"

"I don't know," I said.

"An American?"

"Right. His name is—"

"Why tell me, señor? I only take pictures."

As if to disprove that point, he got a tarp from the trunk of the Seat and rolled what was left of Stu Huntington in it. I helped him tote it to the car. My side ached and my head started spinning. I was suddenly very sleepy. We stuffed the tarp on the rear seat and climbed in front together. The boy had forgotten his camera and had to go back for it. Then we drove into Fuengirola.

The Guardia substation was in a small building a quarter of a mile from the portable bull ring. I was given the freedom of a ten-by-ten whitewashed room. If I wanted to sit, there was a single hard chair. If I wanted to stretch out and catch up on my sleep, there was a bed with a flat spring and no mattress. There was also a small window, barred, and a door, shut and bolted on the other side. I stood at the window and heard a bus roar by in the direction of Gibraltar. A couple of flies buzzed me without any real interest and went back to climbing the walls for the night. A big moth fluttered hopefully but suicidally about the single small bulb dangling on its cord.

Around a quarter after three on my watch, the door opened and a man wearing Guardia gray-greens but no patent-leather hat came in. The black leather holster creaked at his side as he sat on the edge of the bed-spring and lit a cigarette. He was no youngster, but not as old as the guy on the bike. His sleeve was decorated with three stripes. He looked wistful and not tough at all. He looked like Don Quixote without the little pointy beard to give him style.

In excellent English and conversationally he said, "What an awful experience to happen to an American tourist on his first day in Spain. I am Sergeant Martinez, Mr. Drum."

He stuck out his hand. I shook it and said, "I'm no tourist. I'm a private detective."

Sergeant Martinez gave me a wistful Don Quixote smile. "There is no such thing as a private detective in Spain. It is as I said. You are, you see, an American tourist."

"Okay, I'm a tourist. Do I still get to report a murder?"

He stood up, went to the window and gazed out at the silence or listened to the darkness. "Clearly, I failed to understand. You said murder?"

"Huntington was dead before that car crashed."

"He was?" Sergeant Martinez laughed a mild, wistful laugh. "Then where were you driving the body?"

"I wasn't driving. He was."

"A dead man?"

"He was behind the wheel with a dent in the side of his skull. I was sapped and put in the car next to him un-conscious, and then we went for our ride."

"You should not have driven so fast on such a road. The tires. It was a blowout, of course." Martinez scowled. "What does 'sapped' mean?"

"Hit over the head from behind."

"And where did this happen?"

"The cave of Fuentes."

"You went to the cave of Fuentes with the dead man?"

"No. I saw him earlier here in Fuengirola. Arguing

with a man named Fernando. A blind sculptor who lives in Torremolinos."

"Arguing about what?"

"I don't know," I admitted.

"But you knew they were arguing?"

"I heard them and saw them, in a bodega. I didn't hear the words."

"But Mr. Drum, you were seen in the Bodega Costa del Sol with the dead man earlier this evening. Last night, that is."

"Not me."

"You were seen driving off with him."

"I stood up and said, "Hey, wait a minute."

"Facts, Mr. Drum, are facts," Sergeant Martinez said blandly but wistfully. "Why dispute them? Do you still insist Mr. Huntington was dead before the crash?"

"Keep talking," I said.

"Because if he was, and if you were seen with him in Fuengirola earlier, and if indeed the night before you were seen with his wife on the terrace of La Atalaya in Torremolinos, and if she is a woman known to—well, if she were Spanish and a Catholic she would have much to confess to her padre—"

"Spell it out," I said.

"If Huntington were dead before the crash, if he were murdered instead of the unfortunate victim of an automobile accident, if anyone wants to stubbornly insist he had been murdered, we need look no further than this room for our suspect." Martinez said all that to the window. He turned on me to ask, "What were you doing at the cave of Fuentes?"

"Governor Hartshorn of Maryland sent me here to find his son."

"In the cave of Fuentes?"

"In orbit around the moon if that's where he happens to be."

"We of the Guardia Civil will find the missing man. That," Martinez said stiffly, "is our job."

"Like getting to the bottom of a murder is your job?"

"Like investigating an accident is our job." Martinez snickered, managing to make that sound wistful too. "You American tourists. Spain, the land of mystery. Our Moorish blood, the mountains everywhere on a landscape

whose bones protrude like those of dead prehistoric animals, the gypsies, the forlorn wail of a flamenco and the
brave bulls feeding the poor after their moment of truth
on the sand of the arena. Please, Mr. Drum. Things happen
here much as they happen in your country. Accidents
too. Will you be content with that?"

I said nothing.

"What led you to the cave of Fuentes?"

"The last anyone knew, Hartshorn was on his way to
see Ruy Fuentes."

"Why, Mr. Drum?"

"I'd rather not say."

"Very well, don't. After all it is as I have said. You
are no detective here, but only a tourist."

"Yeah, I know. And I was involved in a messy car accident and my driving companion died and if I'm a good
boy you might let me stay in Spain a while longer—say,
long enough to pack my bag."

Martinez looked hurt. "But no, Mr. Drum. Either you
insist foolishly it was murder, and for example see my
superiors in Malaga, in which case we investigate you
and everything about you and probably have you followed and possibly have you denounced; or you recognize
an accident when you see one, as a witness who incidentally was not even in the car, and you are perfectly free to enjoy Spain however you wish. The choice
is yours."

"If I do it your way?"

"I told you. You are free to enjoy Spain. But then
in all truth I would strongly urge you not to return to the
cave of Fuentes."

I didn't ask why. I thought I knew why. He smiled wistfully and I smiled, not wistfully, and said, "Okay, I
won't go jousting with any windmills."

"You know our literature?" he asked, pleased. "Then
perhaps you know *The Four Horsemen* as well? War,
plague, famine and death? Spain is a hard land, Mr.
Drum, and of the four horsemen in the end it is only one
that matters: death. But of course, death no longer matters to its victim. Keep that in mind: death no longer
matters to its victim."

"You mean regarding Huntington?"

"Regarding all the world. It is a truth we of Spain understand."

I was impressed. I have been threatened with guns, knives, forty-watters, blunt instruments and cement boots, but that was the most erudite threat I'd ever received. He had me, though, and the threat wasn't necessary. If I made noises about murder, I could be kept on ice until the bureaucratic wheels went around and around, or maybe regarded as a suspect in the frame he'd started to nail into place before we'd even met. Either way, the best I could hope for was a one-way ticket from Malaga to Madrid and from Madrid to points west. That wouldn't help Huntington; Martinez was right: nothing would help him. But that wouldn't find Robbie Hartshorn either.

"Pues, señor?" Martinez demanded. "Lo que digo o lo que Vd. dice?"

"Huh?" I said innocently. "I'm sorry. I don't have enough Spainsh to read a menu."

"A pity. I asked: your way or mine?"

I said, "It was an accident, sergeant."

"I'm delighted to hear that, Mr. Drum. I like you, but I hope we never have to meet again. You understand?"

I said I understood. I didn't say it was inevitable that we'd meet again, but that was what I thought.

"Adiós, Mr. Drum."

I told him to give my regards to Sancho Panza. He laughed wistfully.

chapter six

If you are a private detective by trade and an international private detective by predilection, you can subscribe to some mighty peculiar journals. The most peculiar one, which got stuffed through the mail-slot of my office door in Washington once every three months, was something called *The Financial and International Black Market Guide*. Few people know of its existence. It is published on Wall Street by a mysterious gent named Axel Spade, who charges fifty bucks for half an hour of his time if you want a personal interview and a hundred and fifty bucks for the four quarterly copies of his magazine. Financial ministries, brokerage houses and international crooks make up most of Spade's subscription list. He has agents all over the world and, sifting the information they send him, he tells his clients and subscribers what they have to know to keep them in business.

If a nation's currency is going to be devalued, somehow Axel Spade finds out before anyone else. If one of the big international cartels is going to split and spin off a multimillion-dollar company, Spade gets wind of it before the directors. If you've sold a shipment of arms illegally to a rebel government in Indonesia, foolishly getting yourself struck with Indonesian currency, Axel Spade will supply the information on what steps you have to take, usually illegal ones, to convert your useless fortune into hard currency that the boys at the Union Bank Suisse won't laugh at. If you want to know what's a good bet to be smuggled where, Axel Spade will tell you. He has committed crimes, technically, in four dozen countries, by acting before the fact with his advice. None of these crimes is sufficient to have him extradited from the United States. Axel Spade has committed no crime in America. He is a cautious man and he loves his adopted country.

When I left the Guardia substation in Fuengirola, I was thinking of Axel Spade and his magazine. About a third of each issue is devoted to what Spade calls *The Smugglers' Newsletter*. About a third of that third is devoted to Spain, because except for the international traffic in heroin, which is almost nonexistent in Spain, the big Iberian country is smugglers' haven. Every black-market item from cigarettes to jewelry to automotive parts will find you an eager buyer in a land where importing duties are prohibitively high, and importing duties are prohibitively high in Spain.

The usual route, Spade has written, is from Gibraltar to the Andalucian coast by fast boat, from the coast to the mountain town of Ronda by burro-train or truck, depending on the size and weight of the contraband, and by any convenient kind of transshipment from Ronda to all parts of the country.

Though they double as rural and small town police, the chief job of the Guardia Civil is to guard against the

entrance and transshipment of contraband. Like cops anywhere, some percentage of the Guardia probably could be
bought. Such as, I thought, my wistful friend Sergeant
Martinez. What would a murder investigation, with the
cave of Fuentes as a focus, mean to Martinez? Why
should it get him all hot and bothered, unless he had
something to lose—such as his cut for keeping the boys
in patent-leather hats off the backs of smugglers who operated out of the cave of Fuentes only a few hundred
yards up from the sea?

I had a few things to go on, more than hunches:
Martinez' repeated concern about the cave and his warning to me not to return there, the truck which had raced
out of the bigger of the two caves and the sapping and
death ride I'd been given because I'd seen it, and the
fact that Robbie Hartshorn had disappeared after visiting the cave. All that and Axel Spade's newsletter too.

I saw Martinez in my mind's eye and smiled his wistful smile back at him. I decided to visit the cave again,
but not yet. First I had to crawl under a blanket and
pull about ten hours of sleep in after me. The obvious
place to do that was where I had dropped the B-4 bag,
at the Hartshorn villa in Torremolinos.

By the time I caught the predawn bus that ran the nine
miles from Fuengirola to Torremolinos on tires as bald as
Yule Brynner's pate, it was almot dawn. I got off just past
the railroad tracks, walked a hundred yards or so and
scowled up at the sixty-three steps leading to La Atalaya.
A rooster greeted the morning with raucous optimism as
I started to climb.

Andrea Hartshorn was waiting for the dawn too. I
found her leaning her elbows on the terrace wall and
gazing out over the red tile rooftops of Torremolinos toward the Mediterranean. She was wearing a black night-
gown and one of those short, quilted bed-jackets with big
buttons that nobody ever fastens. The dawn breeze
whipped her blonde hair about her head. She was smiling
slightly, expectantly. She looked as eager as a kid about
to see her first parade.

"I heard you coming," she said out of the side of her
mouth, not turning her head. "Just a minute. It won't
be long now."

So I got next to her, planted my elbows alongside hers and looked where she was looking. The water was pink and gold, though the sun hadn't risen. I waited. Andrea Hartshorn sighed. All of a sudden a flash of light flamed at the horizon and streaked across the water. It came as quickly as turning on a blowtorch, and the rim of the sun, pink and swollen, followed it. Andrea Hartshorn sighed again.

"It beats electricity," I said.

She just stared.

"So that's what they mean when they say the dawn comes up like thunder out of—"

"Please don't talk about it. You'll spoil it," she said, a little sharply. "I come out and see it every morning. I don't want to share it with anyone."

I could have said she hadn't invented sunrise or something bantering like that. But her intensity got to me: she really wanted that sunrise all for herself. Silly? Some people are like that, and she was a gorgeous dish, so while she looked at the sun I looked at her, and I thought: sunrise and sunset and storms in the mountains and the wonderful wet smell of a forest and the pulse-beat of a city and good music and a walk in the rain and turning to watch your footsteps appear like magic in virgin snow behind you and a roll in the hay—all those things someone who loved her would want to share with her, and if she thought she had a lock on sunrise and you carried it far enough, maybe that was why Robbie Hartshorn put away his quart and a half a day. But then, why did she go and do likewise?

"Learned something last night," I said. "Not much, but it's a place to start."

She whirled toward me as if awakening abruptly from a deep sleep. "You did? I think that's—What on earth happened to you?"

"Does it show? I haven't had a chance to break any mirrors."

"Your suit's all torn. There's blood on your forehead."

"Please don't talk about it," I said lightly. "You'll spoil it."

She laughed, but it took a little effort. "I like you better when you're not trying to be masterful."

I asked, "What did they take away from you when you were a little girl?"

Then she really laughed. "That's the conclusion my analyst finally made me reach, Mr. Drum. But that was a long time ago, and it didn't help." Mocking herself with a bright, bitter smile, she went on, "I was a wide-eyed, trusting kid of five, see? I had a bedroom all to myself just down the hall from my folks' room. Then along came a pink and squealing kid brother, and they turned my room into a nursery and moved him in. I guess it was a tall, skinny house. I had to move downstairs, just down the hall from the housekeeper. I felt rejected, my analyst said. If there's something now I like, I have to keep it private, secret, all to myself. Anybody tries to intrude, he's like my kid brother." She stopped smiling. "I'm as solitary as a cat. I never should have got married."

That wasn't the way she had put it yesterday, but her own special sun had just risen on a new day, hadn't it? She asked, "What did you find out?"

"Robbie saw Ruy Fuentes all right. Ruy lives in a cave with his brother and foster-mother, a gypsy named Maruja. Robbie visited them there."

"You learned all that in one night? Why, that's wonderful. It's more than the Guardia's been able to do in two weeks."

"Mrs. Hartshorn," I said, "did Robbie ever take a flyer in smuggling?"

"Smuggling? I'm afraid I don't understand."

"Well, he wouldn't have had to be a smuggler. In Spain you can buy shares in smugglers' contraband same as you can buy stock shares in New York. You just have to know the right people."

"If Robbie ever did anything like that, he never told me. We certainly don't need the money."

"If he did, would he have told you? Or does he like to have his secrets too?"

"Like a—a private sunrise?" Andrea Hartshorn smiled. "You don't know Robbie. He's just the opposite. Everything he does, he has to tell me. He's like a little boy that way. Maybe it's one reason I love him."

We both stared at the water. I yawned, hurting my left side. "Could I get some shuteye?"

"Forgive me. You have been out all night, haven't you?

One of the maids took your bag into the guest suite. It's yours for as long as you stay. And Chet? I—I want to thank you for reporting what you'd learned to me."

"Hell," I said. "The guy's your husband."

"Yes, but the Governor hired you. I didn't."

I could have said the Governor had hired me out of a sense of obligation and duty, while she loved her husband. I didn't though. If she was as secret and solitary as a cat, and if Robbie had to find approval like a little boy, I had my own cross to bear too. I could get so close to people and no closer. Then this barrier gets in the way. If you want to know why, ask my ex-wife—not that she's anyplace where you could ask her.*

So instead of saying what I could have said, I asked, "Was Tenley out all night too?"

Andrea Hartshorn froze up on me. "What does that have to do with anything?"

"I guess nothing. Well, me for some shuteye."

I went inside and far, far away from her.

If you follow the paving stones of the ramp and steps that lead from the big mill-tower that gives Torremolinos its name down toward the beach, anyone in town will tell you, you'll reach a small adobe house at the bottom of the steps and backing on a stand of rushes beyond which lies the beach and the blue, blue Mediterranean. This was where the blind sculptor Fernando worked and lived with his wife Marcia, North Country by way of Malta, who had swatted Mrs. Stu Huntington in the chops the night before last.

I went down there on foot at about three that afternoon under a sun about as hot as a Mediterranean sun ever gets, which is hot enough for anybody. As I reached the door and mopped my forehead and the back of my neck with a limp handkerchief, I heard the sound of metal striking metal inside. The door was opened by a maid wearing a black uniform and a frilly white apron.

"Francisca?" called North Country from inside the dark, cool house. "Quién es?"

I identified myself and Francisca identified me, and North Country, still in torero pants and still looking

*See *The Second Longest Night* by Stephen Marlowe.

better than six feet tall and this time barefoot, drifted out to squint at me and the sunlight. She had a way of appraising you in absolute silence that was disconcerting, her eyes taking all of you in before she committed herself even to a word of greeting.

"To make up for his blindness?" I asked.

"What? Oh, I see. I never thought of it that way. If you want to know the truth, I think looking at people like that puts them on the defensive."

"Why should you want to put me on the defensive?"

"Francisca said you were investigating the disappearance of Robbie Hartshorn. You scared her by the way, love," said North Country, putting on the broad vowels, I thought, more than necessary. To show me what a simple, uncomplicated type she was? "An investigation in Spain means the police, you see, and there isn't a Spaniard who doesn't fear the police. How can I help you in your investigation?"

"You can invite me in out of the snow."

She laughed, not straining her jaw-hinge but enough to show the joke was appreciated. "It is beastly hot, isn't it? But you should try Malta this time of year."

We went into a large, dark room furnished with heavy pieces as graceful as a spontanato's one and only lunge at his chosen bull. I sat. She sat. Francisca brought me a bottle of San Miguel beer. From somewhere further in the gloom of the small-windowed house came a sound that went *clink, clink, clink.*

"Husband working?"

"He doesn't need light. That's an advantage he has over any other sculptor in a hot climate in summer. He's doing a bronze in *cire perdu.* That means lost wax, Mr. Drum. First he makes a clay model and covers it with a thin coat of wax and covers that with a mold of perforated plaster. Into a furnace it goes, and after the wax melts and runs out through the perforations he pours in molten bronze. Then out comes the statue, the bronze hardens, the plaster is chopped off—and there you have it." I drank my beer. She said, "Dear me, love, am I boring you?"

"I'll bet he wasn't working last night," I said.

"Last night? Why should he have been?"

"No reason at all. I ran into him in Fuengirola, where

he spent some time with Stu Huntington, who was getting red in the face."

"As Stu has been known to get, love. So what?"

"So shortly after that Stu got himself killed."

"Killed?" she squawked, and either it was news to her or she had her guard up as high as the wall around Franco's palace. "God, how did it happen?"

I told her Sergeant Martinez' approved version of the story. She said nothing until I finished, then she bit her lip and said, "No wonder Nancy Huntington wasn't around today. She bothers Fernando all the time, and he's not the only one. She makes it so obvious you'd think she was trying to prove something to herself. But I . . . . shouldn't be talking like this, not with her husband dead, whatever she's like."

"You know any reason why Fernando should have been in Fuengirola with Stu Huntington last night?"

"They often did their drinking together. Here, in Malaga, in Fuengirola, in La Linea across the border from Gibraltar, even in Algeciras sometimes. Fernando needs the stimulus of fresh sounds, he says. They were compatible drinking partners, and Stu often used to chauffeur him around."

"They weren't compatible drinking partners last night."

"I don't see what that has to do with Robbie's disappearance, love, but anyway you'd have to ask Fernando about that, not me."

"He make all his money sculpting?"

"Enough for our needs. He's damned good."

"That's not what I asked. I asked if he made all his money that way."

"He has some investments."

"What kind?"

"The usual kind. Please stop cross-questioning me."

"Smugglers' contraband? That kind of investment?"

"I'll have to ask you to leave."

"Robbie Hartshorn may be in serious trouble," I said. "If he's still alive."

She crossed her legs the other way, her thigh flattening and broadening in the tight stretch fabric of the torero pants.

"You know the Fuentes brothers?" I asked.

"I've seen them fight at the bull ring in Fuengirola."

She had that way of smoothly turning a question away from its target, so I said again, "That's not what I asked. I asked if you knew them."

Silence. Somewhere in the house a faucet was turned on. The clinking sound, which had stopped, was resumed.

"Huntington drove with your husband to the Fuentes' cave before the accident. They parked outside. When the accident happened, Fernando wasn't in the car with Huntington."

"Is that an accusation, love?"

"It's a statement. You husband's a lucky guy."

"It *is* an accusation. Get out of here."

"Okay," I said. "What if I admitted it was an accusation? What if I went further and said there was no accident?"

"You mean Stu Huntington isn't dead?" Relief flooded her eyes. For a moment I thought she would bust out crying, but then her eyes narrowed and she said in a cold rage, "You invented that story, you lied to me just to get me talking?" She stood up, clenching her competent-looking fists to keep her hands from shaking. "Get . . . . out . . . . of here . . . . right now."

"That's not what I mean. He's dead all right. The Guardia call it an accident. I call it murder."

"Fernando!" she bellowed lustily, and the clinking stopped and her husband came out of his studio.

Though he carried no cane and didn't grope with his hands, he walked with the special care of the blind. There was plaster dust on his hands, a white smudge of it on his forehead and more on his black shirt. The tone of his wife's voice had alarmed him.

"Qué pasa?" he asked. His eyes had that pathetically blank look of the blind.

"This man is Mr. Drum," she said in Spanish. "He is a private detective in the United States. He came here to find Robbie Hartshorn."

The blind man's eyes turned in my general direction and stared past my left shoulder. I couldn't pretend a lack of Spanish; I'd spoken it to the maid. He groped for my hand. I shook his. We went through the amenities in Spanish, North Country waiting impatiently. Then she asked, "Did you go to Fuengirola with Stu last night?"

His eyes moved toward the sound of her voice. He didn't answer.

"This man claims he saw you there."

"Then he has an advantage over me. I could not have seen him in any event."

I said, "You and Huntington had some drinks and an argument at a bodega called the Costa del Sol. Then you drove with him in a Lancia sports car to the cave of Fuentes."

His blank eyes could not register surprise. "I deny that."

"Why bother? I saw you there."

He asked, "Is this the way you try to find Robbie Hartshorn, señor?"

"He went to Fuentes' cave too. That's where the trial ends."

The blind man shrugged. "I cannot speak about what I do not know. What is this cave of Fuentes?"

"Among other things," I told him, "a garage—for a truck that had no business there—unless it was loaded to the tailgate with contraband."

He laughed. "Contraband?"

His wife did not laugh. "Stu's dead, this man says."

Fernando laughed again, but not as if he'd heard something funny. "And how did he die, señor?"

"He was killed by a blow to the head. Then he was put in the Lancia, behind the wheel, and it went downhill and finally off a cliff. All this a few minutes after you drove out there with him. Lucky for you you couldn't see it, huh? You're blind. It might have given you a bad night's sleep."

North Country sighed. A muscle twitched on the side of Fernando's jaw. "Exactly what are you accusing me of?"

"That depends on what you did after driving out there with Huntington."

The muscle twitched again. "Be careful," North Country warned me in English. "My husband has a violent temper."

If she was right, that suited me fine. A man doesn't watch his tongue if he has to watch his temper. In Spanish I asked, "Does he get violent enough to commit murder?"

Fernando wore his black shirt with the tails out, and

below that a pair of faded jeans with tool-pockets. He crouched, reached behind himself and came up with a ball-peen hammer coated with white plaster dust. It was big enough, and looked sufficiently deadly in Fernando's hand, to have done the job on Stu Huntington's temple. North Country wasn't kidding. Her husband had a temper all right. No TV cowboy could have drawn his six-shooter, the one with all the notches on the butt, any faster than he drew that ball-peen hammer. He swung it toward the rising inflection of the goading question I'd asked. His aim was good enough to have decorated the floor with a full set of Chester Drum teeth, and then what would have happened to the smile that wins friends and influences people? So I stepped back and to one side, and the hammer only numbed my left shoulder. I grabbed his wrist. North Country shouted something. I twisted, and the hammer fell. Just then there was a knock at the door. The maid, as Spanish maids will, appeared out of nowhere to open it. The blind man shuddered and sighed. I released his wrist.

Silhouetted against the bright sunlight in the doorway, wearing a dress as black as the maid's and no make-up on her face, stood Stu Huntington's widow.

"I didn't know you had company," she said.

"Mr. Drum was just leaving," North Country told her.

Nancy Huntington had developed a shiner that made her left eye look like a purple plum. She seemed to bear no malice toward the woman who had given it to her, and except for her widow's weeds and lack of make-up, she wasn't staggering under the weight of her bereavement.

I rubbed my shoulder. Everybody except Fernando stared down at the ball-peen hammer. "I'll walk you outside," North Country told me.

She did, and in the sunlight said, "When a husband dies, love, and if it's murder or could be murder, where do the police turn automatically for their first suspect?"

I said nothing. I wanted her to say it.

"The wife, love. The wife every time. Don't they?"

"You speaking in generalities, or do you have something to go on?"

"You're the detective, love."

Inside, in her throaty voice I heard Nancy Huntington say, "Stu was in an accident last night. He's dead."

I started up the steps and the uneven paving stones of the ramp, walking gingerly because my shoulder was beginning to throb with pain. I turned once to look back, but North Country already had gone inside. The door stood ajar. The doorway was as black as a hangman's mask.

chapter seven

I took the bus along the corniche road to Fuengirola. It was loaded with Spaniards and expatriates, all heading for the iron bull ring and another afternoon of blood, sand and novilla butchery, the Spaniards looking grim and dedicated, the foreigners happy and relaxed. Except for the rare stranger gifted with afición as the Spaniards feel it, no foreigner understands the awesome tragic beauty of the running of the bulls.

When I pulled the cord to get off on the outskirts of Fuengirola, I drew stares. Except for the driver, who would be shuttling passengers to the bull ring until the blare of the opening trumpet, I was the only one not getting off at the end of the line. Which suited me fine. The chances of running into anyone at the cave of Fuentes were slim. The chances of running into Ruy Fuentes or his picador brother were nil. If I was really lucky I might not be hit over the head with a truck again.

They had removed what remained of the Lancia from the beach. The road and burro-trail were as steep as I had remembered them, and the view of the town and the sea kept changing as I climbed. When I had gone high enough I could see the bus pulled up at the bull ring at the far end of town, disgorging an army of ants.

No signs of life on the burro-trail, nothing sinister, nothing to indicate a man had died here last night. It was just a trail that led past a sheer wall that was part of the Tecada Mountains, and the wall was dotted with the mouths of caves where gypsies lived, and so what if at the end of the trail were two caves that belonged to the brothers Fuentes and the gypsy woman who lived with them?

Big cave entrance and small: it was last night all over

again. I entered the big one, and it was cool and damp as soon as I left the sunlight behind me. I sniffed. It smelled like a garage, which was no surprise.

Ten strides from the entrance, I hit a wall of wood, soft pine in vertical slats with no chinks between them. I explored the edges with my hands. The fit of wood and cave wall wasn't snug, but nothing much bigger than a mouse could squeeze through. I lit a match and did some groping. There were no hinges. I looked up. The barrier of soft pine had been lowered from the roof of the cave like a portcullis. Make something out of that, I thought. There's no law against doors in caves, is there?

I got down on hands and knees, lit another match and groped some more. A padlock joined a thick iron staple at the base of the pine with another staple that had been driven into the floor of the cave: an ideal arrangement for jimmying with a pint-sized crowbar, but I didn't have a pint-sized crowbar or any kind at all. Could I pry the staple out of the soft pine with by boy-scout knife, with which no private detective is ever without? I decided it was possible, and reached into my pocket for the knife.

"Don't move," a voice said in Spanish. "Remain on your knees, señor." The voice belonged to a woman, and it sounded confident enough for me to believe her when she said, "I have a gun. It is pointing at your back. I will use it if you force me to. Now slowly back toward me. No! Still on your knees. Yes, that way." The back of my head tingled. I thought I was in for another sapping.

"I thought all the world would be at the running of the bulls," I said brightly and hopefully in my best Spanish.

"I never go anymore. Not since Ruy was hurt. Who are you?"

"You're Maruja," I said. "I wanted to meet you. Is this far enough?"

"Yes." A hand frisked me calmly and in no hurry. Boy-scout knife and wallet were removed. I could smell her perfume. The base was crushed orange blossoms: it always is. But her scent was more musky than flowery, as befitting a gypsy woman who lived in a cave and sang mournful gypsy songs in the night.

"Ches-tair Droom," she said. "I do not know you."

That meant she was going through the cards in the wallet, and *that* meant she would be having trouble pointing the gun, if any, down at my back. She said, "Why did you wish to meet me?" and I whirled and stood and saw the wallet in her left hand and the gun, a Luger, in her right, close together. She let go of the wallet. I got the Luger. Unlike Fernando and his ball-peen hammer, she didn't struggle to keep possession of it.

"It isn't loaded," she said, and smiled. I yanked the clip from the butt. It was empty. She crouched calmly for the wallet and gave it to me. I slammed the empty clip back into the Luger. She was still smiling. She looked as nervous as a well-fed lioness. For no reason at all I returned the gun to her. She scowled at it, shrugged and threw it away. Literally. It struck the pine boards, hit the floor and bounced against the wall of the cave.

"Why'd you do that?" I asked.

"Of what use would an empty gun be? You wished to meet me, you said. Here we are. Besides, I always do exactly what I wish. I am a gitana—a gypsy."

Nobody, I told myself, was that ingenuous. I gestured at the wall of pine boards. "What's behind it?"

"Who knows?" In Spanish those two words mean more than they do in English. Quién sabe?—some knowledge is difficult and unpleasant, so why bother? "I can guess, though, if you wish. I hear the trucks coming and going in the night, after all. I see the Guardia sergeant climbing the hill once a week for his pesetas. Bah, that pig! With a wife and five children in Fuengirola, and every time we meet he asks me to go to bed with him. 'You are not young, Maruja,' he says, 'and a woman's good years melt away like the snow on the Sierra Nevada in summer.' Bah, that pig!" she said again. "I am twenty-five. Is that old? But if I were forty-five and he were the only man who looked at me that way, it would still be the same. Gitanas are promiscuous, he thinks. He has much to learn. Gitanas sleep with no man who offers himself as a gift. It is the gitana who makes the gift."

She was a gypsy, all right. Not only did she do exactly what she wished, but she said exactly what she wished too. An anthropologist I know in Washington, who works for the State Department, once told me a neurotic gypsy was as rare as a sunburned eskimo. "How could they be neurotic?" he had asked me. "They do whatever they want to do. They are like children without parents to punish them. They don't know the meaning of frustration."

"Let's talk about the cave," I suggested to Maruja.

"Yes, of course. The trucks and the Guardia. Clearly it is a garage and a smugglers' depot. Paco and Ruy, you see, are smugglers. It is no secret in Fuengirola. Half the town knows it."

"Then if somebody stumbled on it," I said, thinking out loud, "that would be no reason to get him out of the way or have him killed?"

"Killed? But señor, of course not." The idea had made her indignant. "Paco and Ruy are good boys. Possibly as a torero Ruy could have earned enough money for our needs. But since his injury . . . . was it not the most natural thing in the world to turn to smuggling? No one is hurt by it. No one loses, except the government tax collector. And merchandise which otherwise would not be available here in Spain is made available. Killed? Mother of God, señor! That is nonsense."

"Then why the gun?"

She shrugged. "With what Paco and Ruy do no secret, what is to stop a thief from coming to the cave and stealing some of the contraband? Would not a merchant's warehouse be guarded? Besides, as you have seen, the gun was not loaded." She asked, "Are you a thief, señor? Is that your intention?"

She was almost too ingenuous to be true, or wanted me to think she was. I said, "A man named Hartshorn came here a couple of weeks ago, to talk to Ruy. He hasn't been seen since. That's why I'm here."

Silence for a few seconds. In the dim light of the cave I hadn't yet seen Maruja's face clearly. Her eyes, though, were enormous, and her voice was deep, musical, very female and as unintentionally seductive as any voice I have ever heard. But now those big eyes narrowed and she hissed at me. "Hartshorn? *Her* father? That one's father? The tall skinny one with no flesh on her bones who chases Ruy so shamelessly? This is who you talk of? Yes, señor. He was here. Borracho, muy borracho. Very drunk, and he wanted to fight. My Ruy was not good enough for his child, he said. Stay away from her, he shouted. Ruy remained calm. Finally he walked down the hill with Sr. Hartshorn. He was afraid the man in his drunkenness would fall and be hurt. He is drunk all the time like all of them, the foreigners of money, in Torremolinos. I do not wish to talk about him."

She flounced out of the cave. I followed her, and she said, not looking back, "Nor do I wish any longer to talk to you—since clearly it is of him and his skinny child you want to speak."

She was small, Maruja the gypsy: in spiked heels she might have been five-three or -four. She wasn't wearing spiked heels. What she was wearing, in ascending order, was a pair of rope sandals, a dark green skirt and a bull-fighter's white shirt that was too big for her and might have belonged to Ruy. Her hair was dark and hung in two thick and glossy braids to her waist. Her hips hour-glassed out from that narrow waist, and she was still mad enough to flounce, making her pelvic sway more pro-nounced and very pleasant on the eyes.

"Let's forget about him and his skinny child," I said. "We could talk about last night."

"Last night?" She stopped walking and turned slowly three strides in front of me. Her brows were thick and naturally arched; she arched them some more, looking her question at me, her big, dark eyes giving me a stare as ingenuous as her attitude had been. One memorable feature and you don't forget a face; for Maruja those eyes would have been enough. But her lips almost made you forget them: full, sensuous lips against the smooth tan of her face, lips as red as the apple Eve gave Adam.

I was staring—and staring too hard—at a very at-tractive woman. Three in one case, I thought; you sure know how to pick them, Drum: Andrea Hartshorn with her blonde good looks, a little the worse for wear, more than a little dissipated; her daughter Tenley, who wryly accepted her own beauty and the fact that men will be men; and now Maruja, as sultry as a summer storm, as uncomplicated as a sudden hunger pang. Or was she? What she did was stare back at me, frankly and with flattering interest, and that is as good a way to change the subject as any I know.

"Guapo!" she cried delightedly. "Oh, but he is guapo! Very handsome and virile-looking, but not a pretty face, I do not like pretty boys. Did anyone ever tell you you have the face of a bullfighter, an old veteran who has slain many bulls and who has felt the horns brush close against his suit of lights. But you are too big, of course. Not ponderous, but still very large. You must be strong, very strong. I can sense it. And guapo? Señor, you delight me." Maruja the gypsy placed her hands on her hips, cocked her head to one side, arched her brows at me and laughed. "But I embarrass you. For a gypsy it is natural to say what she thinks, and when a woman sees a real man . . . . there are so few of them. . . ."

"Look," I said. "Finish the eulogy, and then we can get back to last night."

"Clearly, he is embarrassed. What means this eulogy?"

"Don't know the Spanish word. Forget it."

"This is all you have to say?" She frowned thoughtfully. "Señor, if you slept with a woman, would you be giving a gift or taking one?"

With any woman but Maruja there would have been one sure way, if that was what you wanted, to get back to business in a hurry: by calling her verbal bluff. But Maruja being herself, I should have known better. I would learn. I said lightly, "Why not try it and find out?"

She looked at me gravely. "What is the hour?"

It was four-thirty, and I told her.

"Then still two hours before the running of the bulls is over." She moistened her lips. "Would you wish it? I am ready." To prove that, she closed the gap between us, cried out wordlessly, stood up on tiptoe, threw her arms around my neck and kissed me. Her lips were hot, mobile and alive. Her body squirmed and then nestled. She made a purring sound. Suddenly I had all her weight in my arms. She kissed my chin and the side of my jaw; her tongue touched the lobe of my ear; she kissed my neck. A pulse lurched and throbbed there, where her lips touched.

"Stop biting me," she mumured against my ear. I hadn't been aware of biting her. Probably I had. I can be stirred. "Stop biting me. Ruy will see the mark of your teeth. He would be furious."

That did it. Money or sex, I had told Andrea Hartshorn. But if half of Fuengirola knew the brothers Fuentes were smugglers, how could money be the answer? Which seemed to leave sex. Maruja and Ruy, who she'd cared for since he was a boy? Tenley and Ruy? The missing Robbie Hartshorn and Maruja? He was a pretty virile-looking lad too, and when Maruja offered you her gift you'd have to be an octogenerian monk to refuse— if you took your vows seriously. Maruja and Robbie, and then Ruy breaking it up? Was that what had happened to Robbie Hartshorn?

I disengaged Maruja's arms and placed my hands on her hip-bones to lift her away and set her down on her feet. Back around my neck went her arms. It was like trying to rid yourself of an octopus, so finally I said, "Look, there's Ruy."

She jumped away from me. Except for us, of course, the burro-trail and hillside were deserted. Still, Maruja pirouetted, the green skirt swirling around her thighs, and cried, "Ruy? Where are you? Ruy!" When she got no answer, she whirled back to me. Her eyes were wide and her lips parted. Emotions chased each other across her face: surprise, fear, remorse.

The way she looked took me back more years than I wanted to admit, to a memory I wanted to forget. I'd put up my shingle and waited for the world to flock to the door that said CHESTER DRUM, *Confidential Investigations*. There were a couple of cases, nothing big, and a lot of sitting at a battered old desk and waiting for the phone to ring. The one kind of work, I had told myself there at the beginning, I would never do was divorce work. But the cases did not come and the office rent had to be paid, and the F.B.I. doesn't pension off veterans of a single tour of duty. I knew a guy named Sammy Green who ran a middle-sized Washington agency that made a specialty of divorce work. He used to kid me about being too lily-white to handle his kind of case, and one day over drinks he booted one in my direction. I was hungry enough and disillusioned enough to accept it with thanks. That was the one and only divorce case I ever handled. A surgeon named Burnett or Burdett or something like that was suspicious of his wife. She was earning some kind of advanced degree at Georgetown University, and had to spend weekends out of town to collect data. With one of Sammy Green's photographers along, I tailed her. She was collecting dates, not data, all right. That weekend it was a captain from Andrews Air Force Base. She met him at a motel. I waited for the right moment and, with

Sammy Green's photographer on my heels, busted in the door. The woman sprang out of bed just as the flashbulb went off. The same emotions that crossed Maruja's face had crossed hers: surprise, fear, remorse. Momentarily the surgeon's wife and the gypsy were sisters three thousand miles and all those years apart.

The climax of my one and only divorce case came back to me now as I saw Maruja's face. But if she thought Ruy had returned unexpectedly, why did she look as if her hand had been caught in the extramarital cookie-jar? Ruy wasn't her husband. For ten years she had been a mother to him.

"You lie," she accused me. "Why did you pretend Ruy was here?"

Instead of answering her question, I asked one of my own. "Last night you had some visitors from Torremolinos, didn't you? Here at the cave?"

She shrugged. "Last night Paco and Ruy say it is time for me to visit my cousin, who lives in the fishing village of Carihuela. I spent the night there, with my cousin. It has happened before. I like my cousin."

"What do you mean, it happened before?"

"They have business, Paco and Ruy, with a man from Algeciras who sells shares in smugglers' contraband. Sometimes they go there, but sometimes he comes here. If he does, I go to the house of my cousin in Carihuela."

"You mean all they do is buy shares? Then what's the truck for?"

"I don't understand, señor."

She might or might not have understood, but either way I was puzzled. Buying shares in contraband was exactly like investing in stock. You have nothing to do with the product, except to put cash on the line to purchase some of it in Gibraltar. Then, when the consignment is sold, you reap your share of the profit. But if that was the extent of the brothers Fuentes' involvement, what were they doing with a truck and a warehouse behind a wooden wall in their cave?

"Are they smugglers, or do they just invest?"

Maruja had gained her composure back. She gave me an innocent look. "There is a difference?"

I let that ride. If she was pretending ignorance, there was no point in explaining what she already knew, and if the distinction really didn't mean a thing to her, I'd only confuse her by explaining. I asked, "You know the man from Algeciras?"

"Never have I seen him, señor. But the boys make jokes about him. They call him Pez Espada—Swordfish—as he has a nose like the beak of a swordfish. He owns a bodega on the waterfront in Algeciras. It is no secret. Half of Algeciras knows of his activities in smuggling."

If what she said about Paco and Ruy here in Fuengirola and Pez Espada in Algeciras was true, the movement of contraband along the south coast of Spain was the world's worst-kept secret. As for Maruja herself, she was answering my questions—and they were the sort of questions that could put Paco and Ruy behind bars—without batting an eye. It almost seemed that the smugglers wanted their operations known, and even if they greased the palm of every Guardia from here to Algeciras, that still didn't make sense.

Suddenly I took a stab. "This Pez Espada, was he here the night Robbie Hartshorn came up the hill?"

Maruja scowled. "But no, for then I would have been at my cousin. . . . Wait, I remember. I went, but my cousin was not at home. I returned on the bus, señor. I did not see the man with the nose like a swordfish's beak, but he may have been here. It is usual when I am sent to my. . . ."

Her voice stopped dead. A car was coming up the hill. We stood together silently and stared down the burro-trail until we saw an ancient station wagon with rotting wooden paneling come bouncing along the trail, its engine laboring.

"That is the coach of Dr. Gomez," Maruja cried, and started running down the trail. The wagon came on. She held up one hand and then had to fling herself out of the way. She ran after the wagon in the cloud of dust its tires spun from the parched earth.

The wagon stopped a dozen feet from me. A small bald man got out of the front, went around to the back and opened the tailgate. I stuck my nose in behind him just as Maruja ran up. She took one look inside the wagon and wailed. Two monosabios from the bull ring were squatting in there next to a stretcher on a rack, looking as stolid and poker-faced as monosabios always looked. Kneeling at the head of the stretcher and talking softly to the man who lay there was Tenley Hartshorn. She had a

smile on her face now, but you could see it took effort. She
was pale. There were tears in her green eyes.

The man on the stretcher was Ruy Fuentes. A dark
stain was seeping through his tight torero trousers.

"I can walk," he said gravely, and started to rise to prove
it. One of the monosabios pushed him down.

Tenley said, "Please, Ruy. Don't."

They removed the stretcher from the wagon and carried it toward the smaller of the two cave entrances, the
bald little man leading the way, Tenley on one side and
Maruja on the other. Ruy raised his left hand tenta-
tively. That was the side Tenley was on. She grasped his
hand.

"Pobrecito!" cried Maruja. "Qué pasa? Qué pasa?"

The bald little man, who was Dr. Gomez, said, "Gored,
señora. But not deeply and nothing vital was pierced. A
day or two of rest. . . . the boy is lucky. . . ."

"Pobrecito, pobrecito," wailed Maruja. She leaned
over Ruy. The monosabios had to stop walking. She kissed
his cheek. His face turned toward her. Their lips
brushed and then clung. Ruy let go of Tenley's hand, and
she stared stonily at the top of Maruja's head. The gypsy
woman dropped to her knees and stroked his cheeks and
arms. The kiss was a long one and not motherly. Finally
Maruja stood up. They were at the entrance to the cave.
As if seeing her for the first time, she stared at Tenley.

"What are you doing here?" she said. "You have no
business here."

"Maruja," Ruy pleaded, "the girl is my—"

"The girl is a foreigner and a whore."

Tenley lurched backwards as if she had been struck.
"I'm staying with Ruy," she said, and her voice broke.

"No," Maruja said. "I did not help his father raise him
so that he could fall into the arms of a foreign whore. You
will leave."

Ruy got up on one elbow. His eyes met Tenley's. She
was biting her lip to keep from crying. "Let. . . . Ruy. . . .
decide," she managed to say. She looked pathetically
young and vulnerable.

Pain or pity, or both, twisted Ruy's lips and made him
shut his eyes. "Tenley, Tenley, please try to understand.
Tomorrow I will see you. Or the next day. Now you
must go."

"Ruy, I'll never. . . . if you don't. . . . please, Ruy. . . ."

"You must go now," Ruy said.

And Tenley did, reeling down the trail like a drunk. She could have hurt herself that way. I trotted after her and overtook her. She was crying and running blindly. I took her hand and slowed her down. "You could take a nasty spill."

"I don't care." But she walked at my side and didn't try to run any more. "I never want to see him again." After a few more steps she said, "Yes I do. Oh, I do."

We reached the bottom of the hill. "God," Tenley said. "What kind of hold does that woman have on him? A mother, I could fight that. Or a lover. But both. . . . in the same person?"

I felt sorry enough for her to say, "You may be making too much of that. Could be they have something to hide. That's why they didn't want you inside." Not that I believed it for a minute; they'd let the doctor and the monosabios inside the small cave, hadn't they?

"I saw what I saw," she said bitterly, "and I got told off. Nobody—least of all Ruy—tried to hide that." But she was curious enough to ask, "What are they trying to hide?"

"Same thing your father may have stumbled on. That they're smugglers."

"Smugglers? Ruy? You're crazy." She bristled in defense of him, "He's so honest he wouldn't steal a—a churro if he was starving. Ruy a smuggler! You're crazy."

"Tomorrow I may see just how crazy I am."

We waited for the bus to Torremolinos. It was a long wait in the heat of late afternoon. The bus driver had a seat in the sol at the iron bull ring. Tenley Hartshorn had nothing more to say. I offered to buy her a drink, but she wasn't having any.

Finally we rode back to Torremolinos in the crowded bus. Everybody was talking about the banderillero who had been gored.

chapter eight

From Algeciras you can look across the bay and see the rear view of the Rock of Gibraltar, the view nobody

knows unless he's been there because it hasn't been im-
mortalized by an insurance company.

I got there the next day, taking a bus the seventy-odd
miles along the coast road, past Carvajal and Marbella
and the cork forests between Marbella and Estepona
and La Linea which is the Spanish town at the base of the
Rock. A big American Export liner, white as a ghost,
was anchored in the bay. Its cruise passengers, who had
come ashore on tenders, paraded through the streets of
Algeciras with their cameras, dark glasses and bright
cruise clothing. They clung together in self-conscious
groups, fending off the beggars and peddlers who would
sell them everything from a Swiss watch to the Rock
itself. A lone American sightseer in a foreign port is as
rare as a Southern Methodist with cirrhosis of the liver.

Algeciras was no Torremolinos or Fuengirola. It was
a city of some size and the only deep-water port this
side of Malaga. I checked into the Hotel Reina Cristina
and went down to see the conserje at his desk.

"I'm looking for a bodega," I said.

"On the waterfront there are perhaps thirty that—"

"The one I'm looking for is run by a guy called Pez
Espada."

"Pez Espada?" he repeated. "Swordfish, señor? I know
of no such proprietor of a bodega."

"That wouldn't be his real name," I said, and took one
of Governor Hartshorn's ten-dollar bills from my wallet. "I was hoping you could enlighten me." His stare
moved from the bill to my face and back again.

"But no, señor," he said regretfully. "Truly I do not
know. And if a man called Pez Espada ran a bodega in
Algeciras, I would know."

"Okay. I'd like to buy some shares in smugglers' contraband."

His eyes darted back to the ten-dollar bill. He said,
his lips not moving, "I can arrange that for you."

"I don't want you to. I want to do my own buying—
at Pez Espada's bodega."

He showed me his palms. "But I do not know—"

"Then tell me what bodegas here in Algeciras might
handle it."

He took the ten-dollar bill, studied both sides and let
it flutter into a drawer on his desk. "Almost any one

of them," he said slowly. "You see the barman and tell him you are interested in a shipment of goods consigned from Gibraltar to Malta."

"That's all?"

"Sí, señor."

"You earned an easy ten bucks."

I started walking across the lobby. A woman seated on a chair and with her face hidden behind a copy of the Paris edition of the *Herald Tribune* said, "Ruy used to mention a man named Pez Espada to me."

She folded the paper. It was Tenley Hartshorn.

"He did?"

"Sure, lots of times. Pez Espada was Ruy's teacher when Ruy was studying to be a bullfighter. Is he supposed to be a smuggler too?"

"That's the way I hear it. What else do you know about him?"

"He owns a big bull-breeding ranch, or did, in Ronda. That's about all. Some smuggler."

"What are you doing here?"

"Following you, Mr. Detective. Andrea said you were coming to Algeciras. I missed the bus and borrowed her car. Knowing you were on my grandfather's expense, the Reina Christina seemed the right place to look," she said sarcastically.

"And now that you're here?"

"Can I come with you—looking for Pez Espada?"

"Don't be silly," I said.

"Wait, please. It's very important to me. You—you're not that dumb. If Ruy is a smuggler, I want to know it. If that had anything to do with my father's disappearance, I want to know it. If—" she moistened her lips "—you can show me Ruy's not the knight in shining armor I always thought he was, maybe that would help me. Please can I go with you?"

"You'd better not. Who knows what I'll be walking into?"

She retreated behind a forced smile. "Well, Andrea always told me not to be forward with strange men."

I left. At the door I turned and saw her staring after me.

The first bodega I hit was a place called *La Estrella*

de Algeciras. It was still too early in the afternoon to be crowded. A few fishermen were buying wine for a pair of sailors off the American Export liner, and a middle-aged cruise passenger, flanked by two other middle-aged cruise passengers who were giggling, was having her caricature drawn by a ferret-faced artist with a brown-paper cigarette stub pasted to his lips.

I ordered a sherry at the bar and told the barman, "I'm interested in a shipment of goods consigned from Gibralter to Malta."

He did not look surprised. "How interested?" he asked.

"Five hundred dollars American. A thousand, if I like the consignment."

"You would never see it, señor."

"The manifest, then."

"Nor that either. Unless it was two thousand. Or unless you were a steady customer."

"Well, I could go as high as two thousand—if a man called Pez Espada handled it for me."

"Swordfish? I know of no such man." He seemed genuinely puzzled. "If a man who calls himself Swordfish was in this business that—interests you, señor, I would know it."

I believed him, and I was as puzzled as he was. I paid three pesetas for my sherry and headed back through the narrow barroom toward the door. The caricaturist had finished his sketch. "Señorita, you like a picture?" he said in English, facing the doorway.

Tenley Hartshorn was standing there, her big green eyes looking grave. She drew stares. Being Tenley Hartshorn, she would, and because she was used to it that made her smile a little. "No, thank you," she said.

I reached her. "Well, well. Looks like I had a tail. Pretty good one too. I never spotted you."

"Better not say that. I might cable the Governor, and he'd take your expense account away." She bit her lip. "I didn't mean to say that. It just came out. I want to be friends. And I still want to come with you."

I still would have said no, had there been any suggestion of hanky-panky or danger in that first bodega. But the barman had accepted my offer to invest in contraband so matter-of-factly, except for my mention of Pez Espada, that I saw no possibility of Tenley involving herself in anything more deadly than too many sherries. Besides, I was feeling sorry for her, and when you start feeling sorry for a beautiful girl, half her battle's won.

"I don't want to drive back to Torremolinos telling myself I could have learned something and didn't. Please?"

So I shrugged and said, "Okay, what the hell. Make like my Girl Friday."

She smiled, and it wasn't forced. She took my arm and snuggled up to me on the way out.

chapter nine

A private detective hitting the bars, even if they're in Spain and called bodegas, is like a cop hitting the flats in search of information. After enough of it there is too much stale air, too many cigarettes, too many drinks you don't taste, too many weary and unsurprisable faces over unsteady hands polishing the same glasses over and over with a dirty dishrag. Then one day you sit on the edge of an uncomfortable bed in a nameless hotel in a distant city, and you tell yourself: hell's molten bells, a hundred thousand cigarettes and ten thousand shots of whiskey (or sherry) and flat feet and that hair is starting to go salt-and-pepper on you, buddy, and what do you have to show for it but a clever line of chatter and a lot of loneliness which it hides and not quite enough money in the bank to pay for a trip to all those places you never really saw because you were too busy hitting the bars (or bodegas) to collect your hundred bucks a day and expenses.

I wanted to avoid that moment of truth. Tenley wanted to find out something about herself by finding out something about Ruy. We're all of us human. I took her with me.

She was a girl who could throw herself into fun the way a diver plunges off the high board. Under the circumstances I hadn't expected that, and it surprised me. In the first bodega we hit together, gypsy dancers were stamping and clapping their disturbing flamenco rhythm. We had a couple of drinks, and before I dropped my question in front of the barman Tenley found the rhythm with her own hands. She clapped it out, softly and then louder, and pretty soon she was on her feet and dancing, her body very straight, just her feet moving, until the two men among the gypsies came over and, looking down at her gravely and with approval, stamped their slow, provocative dance around her. She had a pair of castanets then; I don't know where she got them but she knew how to use them. She danced faster and the gypsies danced faster and the guitar kept pace and everybody in the bodega was smiling at her, even the gypsy women who were sitting this one out on hard chairs on either side of the old guitarist. Finally it was over, and one of the gypsy women shouted, "Olé! Olé!, gitana brava!"

I dropped my question. The barman had never heard of Pez Espada. We got out of there. Tenley held my hand and squeezed it. I could feel a pulse throbbing in her fingers.

In another bodega, where the answer to my question again was no, we met the same caricaturist who'd done the cruise-passenger's portrait. He offered to do Tenley's, but she shook her head, then suddenly smiled, stood up, gestured to her chair, took sketch pad and chalk sticks from him, reached into his breast pocket for the brown-paper cigarettes, stuck one between her lips, lit it, squinted through the smoke and began to do his portrait in bold strokes. A crowd gathered to watch. She caught the ferrety look on his face perfectly, finished the caricature off with a cigarette pasted to his lips and gave him the result. He stood up and bowed, not mockingly. Everybody applauded. The artist was impressed, they were impressed and so was I.

Later, in another bodega, we were dancing a slow pasa doble on the small, crowded floor. They never gave me any medals at Roseland, but I don't have two left feet. Tenley danced close, looking up at me dreamily. I could feel the rhythm in her slender, lithe body. With her in my arms on a crowded dance floor I was my generation's answer to the ageless Fred Astaire, and I knew it would be that way for anyone dancing with her.

"There anything you can't do?" I asked.

She'd had her share to drink but seemed to be holding it. "You mean like with the artist and the gypsies?"

"Uh-huh."

"Too many boys I've dated would think that's in poor taste. They'd get a sick smile pasted on their faces while pretending to enjoy it. Nuts to them." She said nothing about Ruy. "But you're different. I can enjoy myself with you, and all of a sudden I want to." She smiled up at me dreamily again. It was her answer to Ruy and Maruja.

By the time we reached a bodega called *La Perla,* shortly after ten that night, Tenley had—in her words —a man-sized buzz on. She wasn't looped, but skidrow bums with empty bottles of Sneaky Pete had been so- berer. In the last few places I'd ordered clams and shrimps for her, and tried to taper off her drinking. There was an end-of-the-world frenetic quality about her that really socked me.

La Perla wasn't crowded. Dinner hour in Spain arrives indolently after the paseo, and on a warm summer evening the paseo lasts until ten o'clock. A couple of drunks at the bar were arguing over a lottery ticket; except for them and the barman we had the place all to ourselves.

I asked my question, which evoked the usual mild in- terest, and when I was told I couldn't see the manifest on my investment under two thousand dollars, I said I'd go that high if Pez Espada was the middleman.

The barman was fat and had a scar to one side of his mouth that puckered like a dimple when he smiled his lazy smile. "Who, señor? Say that again."

"I'd go to two thousand or even higher if Pez Espada was the guy who handled the dinero."

"That is what I thought you said. Will you wait, señor? For favor?"

I said I would wait. The barman lumbered through a curtained doorway at the rear of the bodega.

"Think you struck paydirt?" Tenley asked.

"Maybe."

"Suddenly I'm scared."

The curtains parted and the fat barman stepped through. "If you will come this way, señor?"

"Stay off the sauce," I told Tenley. "It will only give you Dutch courage and a hangover."

"I'm all right now."

I got up and walked back past the drunks to where the

barman was waiting. He parted the curtains for me and followed me through them to a dim hallway lit by a single naked bulb dangling from the ceiling. At the far end was a door.

"It is not locked," the barman said behind me.

It wasn't. I started to open it. I should have been thinking of Pez Espada, but I was thinking of Tenley.

Something exploded against the base of my skull and white lights danced a flamenco in front of my eyes. I lurched a step. My head butted the door open. I went to hands and knees on a cool terra-cotta tile floor. Bile in my throat made me gag. I looked along the tile with interest but no great enthusiasm and saw the legs of a chair, the legs of a man and the legs of a desk. I dragged myself toward the chair. Maybe it would be a nice chair and help me get back on my feet. The door shut behind me. Footsteps. That would be the barman. The place was full of legs.

"Get up," a voice said in Spanish.

The barman got hold of my left arm and helped me. He sat me roughly in the chair. Either it groaned or I did. The barman stood behind the chair. A man I had never seen before stood to my right. He wasn't big, but he looked tough in that grave and untheatrical way only a Spaniard can look tough. The chair was facing the desk, behind which sat a man, middle-aged and middle-sized, gray-haired or sandy, neither big nor small-boned, not very fair-skinned for a Spaniard and not particularly dark for anyone else, a man as nondescript as any old white-washed wall in any old whitewashed town along the Costa del Sol—except for his nose. It was a long nose, a very long nose almost like Cyrano's, and it tapered the way a nose usually doesn't. I thought it would quiver when he spoke, and it did. He said, "Tell me what you know about Pez Espada." His voice was any man's voice. His Spanish was neither Castilian nor Andaluz.

"That's easy," I said. "One look at you is all anybody needs. You're Pez Espada."

"I could hurt him again," the barman suggested behind me.

Pez Espada shrugged. "Not yet. Perhaps not at all. You have already demonstrated that he comes in here with no rights and no hopes except the rights and hopes we grant him."

"But if he has fear now, and if I can increase that fear. . . ." the barman suggested hopefully.

"Shut your mouth, Estebán," the tough-looking Spaniard growled. "The señor is talking."

The señor said, "You are American? Or English? But who you are, or what you want with Pez Espada, that we do no know."

I told him my name. I said he was right the first time: American.

"Let me see your wallet."

"Why should I? I come in here to invest in some contraband, and first I get slugged from behind and then the fat boy here makes some threats which, incidentally, will earn him a broken arm if he tries to carry them out. Would you like to count my teeth too? I'm not selling anything, Swordfish. I'm buying."

"Why buy from me?"

"I was told you were reliable as they come."

"Yes, and who told you that?"

"In a bodega in Torremolinos they told me."

Pez Espada smiled a little and said, "Hurt him again, Estebán."

I stood up fast, pushing the chair back. It caught the fat man in his fat gut, and he bent over it. I judo-chopped the back of his neck. He and the chair fell down, making a racket they would have heard across the bay in Gibraltar. I saw a blur out of the corner of my eye. The tough Spaniard was moving, and moving too fast for me to stop him. What he did was get hold of my hair and yank my head way back and with his free hand jab two outthrust fingers at my Adam's apple. I grabbed my throat. I couldn't breathe. The chair on the floor or the fat man, or both, tripped me. I joined them on the tiles. When I could breathe again, a little, it was like inhaling the flame of a blowtorch. I started to get up and heard running footsteps, light and click-clacking on tile: a woman.

Tenley leaned over me and said something indignant. I was still concentrating on the difficult job of breathing. The fat man sighed and stirred himself. Then he saw me and reached out for me, but grabbed Tenley's leg instead. She tried to shake loose and wound up kicking him in the head, not hard. He yanked at her leg and she fell heavily. Then I kicked the fat man in the ribs, hard. He screamed like a woman and clutched his side. One of the drunks from the bar looked in through the doorway, a foolish grin on his face. The tough Spaniard just stared at him and he left in a hurry.

I helped Tenley to her feet and set the chair upright. She sat on it. The tough Spaniard shifted his stance to face me menacingly, light and ready on the balls of his feet.

"That's enough," Pez Espada said. He hadn't moved from the desk. Why bother? Now he was holding a revolver in his hand.

The fat man got up, listing like a ship with a hole in one side under the waterline. "The bar," Pez Espada told him. "Possibly there are customers. Possibly you'll be able to handle them." The fat man swayed to the doorway and through it, clutching his side. The tough Spaniard shut the door after him.

"What will the gun get you?" I asked Pez Espada.

"Except for the fat one and Diego here, only a handful of people call me Pez Espada. Is that not true, Diego?"

"Is true, señor," said Diego.

"One of them told you about me," Pez Espada went on. "I wish to know which one—and why."

"Hell," I said, "I was trying to make a contact. I've got some money. I want to invest it in contraband."

"You could have done that almost anywhere in Algeciras. Why come to me?"

"Because I'd want to know what I'm buying."

"But you'd be buying nothing. Only investing."

I said, "Like Paco and Ruy Fuentes only invest?" Tenley held her breath.

Pez Espada looked at Diego, who shrugged. "You interest me," Pez Espada said. "But I cannot believe the brothers Fuentes told you about me."

"I can't believe their business is only buying shares of contraband—not with the truck they run out of Fuengirola.

He didn't want to talk about that, but he picked up my lead. "Then you also wish to—more than invest?"

"Now you get the idea. If you set them up, I figured you could set me up."

"You have a boat?"

"I can get one."

"And a Gibraltar export license?"

"I can get one. I'd have to see how it works."

"Why should I show you?"

"For a percentage. You name it."

"A third," he said, "and the exclusive right to sell shares in your cargo."

"You'd have me all tied up."

"You do not operate on this coast without being all tied up."

"And I'd deliver my cargo to the Fuentes brothers?"

He smiled. Diego almost smiled. "If you know so much, why ask me?"

"Maybe," I said, "that was Robbie Hartshorn's trouble."

Again Tenley held her breath. "Quién?" said Pez Espada. "Who?"

I repeated Tenley's father's name. If it meant anything to him, he did a fine job of hiding the fact. "I am sorry," he told me. "I do not understand."

"Then forget it. Suppose I just invested—right now, tonight. Who'd be running the cargo from Gibraltar?"

"A competent man. Or I would not be his broker."

"Would he mind competition from me?"

"He is not the only captain for whom I am broker."

"Good," I said. "That's what I'm after. There room for another?"

"There is always room for a good man. May I see your seaman's papers?"

"They were lifted in the States. I had some trouble," I improvised, "running rum from Puerto Rico to the mainland."

There was a silence. Pez Espada put his gun away. He broke the silence by saying, "Two thousand dollars."

"What for?"

"An investment. Then you can meet the captain. Perhaps he'll take you along. Then he'll report to me, and then we can discuss further business."

"Perhaps my foot," I said. "You tell him and he'll do it."

"Perhaps," Pez Espada said again, and waited.

I slipped my shirttails out of my pants, unzipped a compartment of my moneybelt and took out a wad of Governor Hartshorn's money. They were crisp new fifties, folded once the long way. I counted our forty and dropped them casually on Pez Espada's desk. He didn't touch them.

"Where can I contact you, Señor Drum?"

"The Reina Cristina."

"Await word from us there."

"Diego opened the door. When I reached the bar with Tenley, fat Esteban sneered at me. "Wipe it off your face, Fat One," I said. "One of these days you may be taking orders from me."

"Cojones," was his answer.

Outside, Tenley asked me, "Are you satisfied with the way it went?"

"How do you mean?"

"I mean you didn't have much convincing to do. After showing you how tough he could be, the man with the nose seemed mighty eager to please. And—and apparently Ruy is a smuggler. Isn't that lovely?"

I ignored her remark about Ruy. "Listen," I said, "I'm looking for your father, remember? Say he stumbled into something he shouldn't have at the cave. Maybe I'll find out what it was if I dig out the real relationship between Pez Espada and the cave in Fuengirola."

"Then you didn't believe him?"

"Of course not. He doesn't know one damn thing about me. Why should he have offered to take me on?"

"Then what—?"

"He wants to get me together with this captain of his. I'm curious enough to want to know why."

"Be careful," Tenley said, and squeezed my arm. "You and the cat."

chapter ten

Nobody contacted me that night or in the morning. Tenley and I spent the morning on the breakfast terrace. She wanted to talk about anything that had nothing to do with what she really wanted to talk about. She was friendly and gay, but her smile was brittle. So we talked about this and that and once she started to talk about Maruja and Ruy. She stopped that in a hurry, but for the next hour she was holding my hand and making big green eyes at me.

"Like some lunch?" I asked.

She nodded, and we had it in her room—tuna steak, salad and a good white wine. We had a second bottle of the wine, and conversation flowed as freely. After a while Tenley went into the bathroom and changed into a bikini consisting of two polka dot handkerchiefs. She picked up the second bottle of wine. "Me for the terrace and some sun." She was a little drunk and wanted to be more drunk than she was. Up-ending the bottle, she drank from it. Then she whirled and asked, "Do you like my body? He used to say he wished he was a painter so he could put it on canvas and have it all the time. I'll bet he's told that to . . . . Maruja too."

She went outside on the terrace, equipped with a towel and the bottle. Pretty soon she called, "Chet?"

I wandered out there. She was lying face-down on the towel. The bottle was empty, the sun dazzling and the up-stairs handkerchief of the bikini unfastened. I liked her body, all right.

She said nothing. I said nothing. I began to sweat in the sun and for other reasons. "What does a gal have to do?" she mumbled into the towel. She wiggled her hips a little and stretched her arms.

"Don't say it," I said.

"Do I have to *say* it?"

"You have to mean it. And you wouldn't."

"All right. I'll say it. I'm light as a feather. Take me inside and put me on the bed and don't close the shutters unless you're a very low-class type—which you aren't."

I went on sweating.

"Come here. I dare you to touch me."

"What would that be doing," I said, "except getting even on him for something you don't quite understand."

"I understand all I want to. But I had to pick a man with moral scruples." She buried her face in the towel and started to laugh. I went over there, crouched and touched her shoulder. She was shaking. She spun into my arms, sobbing. I lifted her and she clung to my neck and right arm, her head flung back, her eyes shut and tears trickling down her cheeks. Her breasts were firm and like ripe, red-tipped fruit.

I carried her inside. She was right—light as a feather. I put her on the bed. She smiled up at me with her eyes still shut and the tears still coming.

"Do it," she said. "Do it to me now."

Instead I covered her with the sheet.

"What's the matter, don't you want me?"

"I want you," I said in a funny voice. "You're beautiful. I'd have to be a eunuch not to want you. What does that have to do with anything?"

Then she really started to bawl, covering her face with the sheet. Her voice came through it, muffled, "If I . . . .want you and you . . . . want me, damn it, why do I still . . . .love him?"

I stayed with her, sitting on the edge of the bed, until she cried herself to sleep.

The call came a couple of minutes before five o'clock. By then I was stretched out on the bed in my room, chain-smoking and staring at the ceiling. I'd taken a long, ice-cold shower and was telling myself that and the fact that I was a noble son of a bitch more than made up for what I'd turned down in Tenley's room. Telling myself that and not quite believing it, and then the phone rang.

"This Drum?"

I said it was.

"MacPherson's the name. Señor Manzanarez tells me I need a supercargo tonight."

"Señor who?"

"Manzanarez. You kidding or something? Manzanarez the broker."

Which was what Pez Espada was called when he wasn't called Swordfish. "Keep talking," I said.

"It ain't my idea," MacPherson said. "I need a supercargo like I need a hole in the brain-pan. But if Manzanarez gets the dough and puts it up, who am I to gripe? Well, the boat's at pier three on Gib. Ask anybody there for MacPherson. My papers read Malta," he said, and laughed. "They always do. I'll be casting off at nine-thirty."

He hung up before I could say I'd be there.

I looked in on Tenley. She was sleeping like a baby who had cried too much. I wrote her a note on Reina Cristina stationery, saying the contract had been made and I'd see her back in Torremolinos. I didn't say when because I didn't know when.

The afternoon launch took me across the bay to Gibraltar. I showed my passport and climbed the hill and prowled the main drag, which looked shabby and run-down like any main drag in any British colonial port I have ever seen. About eight-thirty I made my way back down the hill to the harbor, where MacPherson and a boatload of contraband were waiting.

Lights were coming on along commercial mall when I got there. A big four-engined turboprop took off from the nearby runway, Gibraltar's one and only, that bisects the isthmus connecting the Rock with the Spanish mainland at La Linea. When its banshee whine had faded, the pier three watchman unclamped his teeth from the stem of a curved briar, scratched behind his right ear with the mouthpiece and said, "MacPherson, is it? And you'd be going to Malta?"

"If that's where MacPherson's going."

He thought that was very funny. "That's where Mac-Pherson always goes, laddie. Or so he says. What's your name?"

"Drum."

"You're expected. She's over there, the *Marbella Lady*. Funny name for a boat that plies between Gib and Malta, now isn't it?" He laughed and sucked at his pipe again.

Marbella Lady was a forty-foot inboard cruiser with a flying bridge. She sat high enough out of the water to make me wonder if the contraband had been loaded yet.

"Ahoy, *Marbella Lady*," I called. Nobody seemed to be aboard.

The cockpit hatch opened, and a tall figure loomed. "Come aboard, Drum."

"Captain MacPherson?"

He nodded. He was as tall as Paco Fuentes but as gaunt as a gallows. In the glow shed by the pier lights his face was all angles and hollows. The two deepest hollows hid his eyes. He was wearing an old yatchman's cap crushed out of shape. I offered my hand to shake, but he declined it with a sour grunt.

"She's sitting pretty high," I said in a friendly tone. "What are you running, a boatload of air?"

"Hot air I don't need from you, friend."

"So that's the way it is," I said. "I guess I don't say pleased to meet you. I guess I put on my brass knucks Estepona last month. Can you use a rifle?"

"Well what the hell did you expect?" he said. "I told you on the phone I got no use for a supercargo. Manzanarez wants me to take one, I play ball. I don't have to like it. Where does your cut come from, friend?"

"Didn't Manzanarez say?"

"Manzanarez said he was sending along a super on account of there's been lots of highjacking along the coast lately. Christ, don't I know it! I got my cargo lifted off Estepona last month. Can you use a rifle?"

"Sure. What do you think Manzanarez sent me along for?"

That was a mistake. MacPherson said, "In a pig's ass. Manzanarez says we start shooting along the coast, we bring the Guardia. They're paid off to keep their distance, unless we make like the Fourth of July. The rifles, they're my idea, not Manzanarez'. So now I'll ask you: what did Manzanarez send you along for, friend?"

"Maybe he's worried about you and your rifle."

MacPherson grunted again, sourly again. "Maybe. I told him. If I get highjacked I don't get paid, and if I don't get paid I been working for nothing. But get this straight, friend. If it happens tonight like it happened last month, and if you try to stop me, the first slug's for you. It's a Weatherby Magnum .300 and if you know your way around rifles I don't have to tell you it can blow your goddam head off."

I said nothing. He asked, "Well, did he or didn't he send you along to hold my hand in case of trouble?"

"I'm thinking of making the run myself. I wanted to see the setup. That's why Manzanarez sent me along."

"Why didn't you say so in the first place?"

"I said I wanted to see the setup. Seeing how the possibility of highjackers makes your ulcer gnaw away at you, that's part of the setup."

"Scared?"

"Uh-uh. Curious. Also about the cargo. What is it?"

"You could be customs."

"Sure," I said. "Since when do the Gib customs people bother you? You're not breaking any British laws. Besides, Manzanarez told you to reach me at the Reina Cristina, didn't he? And I was there, wasn't I? Leave your ulcer alone, MacPherson. It'll dig a hole all by itself."

"What have you got to back up those wisecracks, friend?"

I shrugged. MacPherson was a guy who had to make a conversation an argument, just as I was a guy who had to crack wise in front of a sourpuss. I said, "You can always decide to find out."

He looked at me a while and backed off. "I got enough worries as it is."

"What's the cargo?"

"Cigarettes," he grunted. "American. Ships' stores in waxed cartons. They're a buck-eighty a carton aboard ship and at PX's in North Africa. We get them for three-sixty a carton, we deliver them for six bucks a carton, and they sell in Spain for fifty-five pesetas a pack. That's ninety cents, friend. I'm carrying six brands, three hundred cartons each. So my net ought to be forty-three hundred smackers minus operating costs, but it ain't, not by a long shot. I usually put up cash for half the consignment, and Manzanarez sells shares for the other half. Then he lifts a third off the top of my half, and then I got to grease the Guardia's palms. Me, I'm lucky if I come out of it with a stinking five-hundred clams."

"That's not bad for a night's work."

"Not ulesss the boss thinks you're a troublemaker. And not unless—"

"Manzanarez thinks you're a troublemaker?"

"Sure. I told you. He don't like me to run the stuff armed. And he don't like it, me telling some of the other boys to do likewise."

"You're still in business. It's still pretty good for a night's work."

MacPherson was still unhappy. He said, "Not if you got to worry about highjackers it ain't."

We were running in a smooth black sea about two miles off the coast on an easterly course. In a calm sea, *Marbella Lady* could make fifteen knots. By two-thirty that would have put us off Fuengirola. For four and a half hours I'd had nothing to do but listen to MacPherson's morose account of his line of work and to the throbbing roar of the big inboard engine. But at two-thirty MacPherson cut our speed to half and said complainingly, "Wouldn't you know it? Clouds I can do without. We lay off running lights, we can use a moon."

There was no moon. There were no stars. A solitary light showed on shore occasionally to let us know the world was still there. We could see each other faintly in the glow from the instrument panel.

"We heading in?" I asked. "Where do we land?"

"Nowhere. We stand off shore and get met by a couple of skiffs."

"Where?"

"What's the dif where?"

"We ought to be close to Fuengirola," I said.

"Know the coast, huh?" MacPherson said grudgingly.

"Who picks the stuff up, the Fuentes boys?"

He seemed genuinely surprised. "Fuentes? I never heard of them."

Running at half speed, *Marbella Lady* turned in a wide arc toward the coast. MacPherson lit a cigarette. Then, because at half speed *Marbella Lady* ran quietly, I heard it. The roar of another powerful engine off somewhere in the darkness.

MacPherson heard it too. He cut our own engine, and *Marbella Lady* drifted in the night. Somewhere ahead of us a light burst dazzlingly on the darkness. A big searchbeam probed across the water toward us, low, touching the calm sea with gold. It swung starboard and then came back. It held us. The roar of the engine grew louder.

"Christ, it's them!" MacPherson cried.

"Can you outrun them?"

"I tried that," he said bitterly, "last month. They can make twenty knots and they got that light. But last month I didn't have my Weatherby. Last month I hove-to and they shut their light and came aboard and took the stuff. I never even saw their goddam faces."

MacPherson laughed nervously. "This time we got a surprise for them." Whatever his surprise was, he was in no hurry to spring it. The light was close and coming closer. He said, "You told me you could handle a rifle. Now prove it." He left the instrument panel and returned with a bolt-action Weatherby rifle. "Here you go, friend. Shoot out that goddam light. The minute you do, that's when we start running."

I went out on deck with the Weatherby. A faint off-shore wind was blowing. The sea was flat and calm. The light grew bigger, brighter. I worked the rifle bolt, drew the butt of the stock against my shoulder, took a breath and held it, and fired. The Weatherby roared. It had a kick like a hopped-up burro.

The light splintered, fragmented and was gone.

Marbella Lady's engine sprang to life. MacPherson shouted something. We turned fast and I almost pitched overboard. Then we were running straight. I returned to the cockpit. MacPherson was pleased with himself. He was chuckling.

"You knew how to use it all right," he said.

And then a big fat Mediterranean moon peeped out from behind a bank of clouds.

Seconds later there was a chattering, bursting roar behind us. I whirled to stare out the open door of the cockpit. MacPherson began to curse.

They had a machine gun, and they were using it—tracer bullets and all. The tracers made quick leaping arcs low across the water. Too far to port, and then closer and then on target.

MacPherson cut the engine a second time. "Christ, we can't mess with that," he said.

We were drifting. The machine gun's busy chattering roar stopped. So did the other boat's engine. I could see it in the moonlight as it drifted up. It looked like a high-powered fishing boat, ungainly and ponderous, the kind they said out of the southern Spanish ports. It had two masts but no rigging. It didn't need rigging. With its big engine it could overtake a swift cruiser like *Marbella Lady*.

When it drifted close, a voice hailed us in Spanish, "Walk aft! No weapons! Hands high where we can see them!"

MacPherson obediently put his hands up and left the cockpit. The machine gun had ripped his courage to shreds. I couldn't blame him.

"Just take it easy now," he told me. "All them bastards want is the cargo. A machine gun," he mused. "Christ, they never had a machine gun before."

That should have warned me, but I was playing it by ear. I followed MacPherson aft, my hands raised.

"Hijos de la gran puta!" he shouted. "You can board."

Instead, very close, the machine gun roared and chattered deafeningly. It was set up on their foredeck, not fifty feet from us now. I dove for the deck and shouted a warning to MacPherson—too late. I could see the angry orange path of tracers disappear into his body. He danced wildly backwards, crashing against the cockpit bulkhead. He actually made it to his feet once. The tracers found him again. They stitched into his neck and head. Glass shattered behind him. He went down a second time. He would have to wait for Gabriel's trumpet to rise again.

The night was suddenly silent, except for the lapping of water against our lapstreak hull. Since diving for the deck, I hadn't moved. The other boat drifted closer, I could hear voices, and they weren't shouting.

"You think both of them?"

"I don't know."

They were talking Spanish.

"Give them some more to be sure."

The machine gun roared, very close. They didn't want our cargo. Or maybe they did. What difference did it make? The main thing they wanted to do was kill us. Wood splintered all around me. I told myself as soon as the machine gun stopped I would get up and dive overboard and stay under as long as I could, swimming, and then surface for air and then go under again and swim again.

But first there was the fear. I could smell it in the stench of cordite, they were that close. I could taste it in my mouth. I could feel it on the deck-planking, wet with MacPherson's blood. I could feel it too whenever wood splinters flew close to my face or against it. All I could do was wait. They were riddling the boat. I was sure they would get me. For no reason at all I thought of Tenley Hartshorn. She would have been magnificent in bed.

The machine gun cut off. I was drenched with sweat and shaking. I was as limp as MacPherson's bullet-riddled body. There was a thump, and another. They were fending off from us. It was dark then. The moon had drifted behind clouds again. I heard a thud, and the cruiser rocked slightly. A big man had jumped aboard. He missed me in the darkness, but he would be back. Faintly I could see him as he moved forward to MacPherson's body. He crouched over it, grunting. Then he started coming back. The way he held one arm out in front of him probably meant he had a gun. I couldn't be sure in the darkness. He was big enough, but not fat: he could have been Paco Fuentes. I couldn't be sure of that either.

He came close. His shoe prodded me. He wouldn't be sure either, not unless he examined me, not unless he felt for a pulse or listened for a breath. I had MacPherson's blood on me, but with MacPherson he could have really told. MacPherson must have been hit by fifty slugs. Half the bones in his body must have been smashed.

The foot prodded me again. He might just decide to shoot. Why bother examining me? They weren't stingy with ammunition, were they?

I grabbed his leg and yanked as hard as I could. The gun went off. He shouted. I rolled and got to my knees and still rolling went over the side. I went under. The water was cool. I floated down in darkness until pressure hit my ears. Then I drew my legs up and removed my shoes, and then I started swimming. Toward shore? Away from it? I didn't know. I'd lost my sense of direction.

My lungs began to feel like lead. I had to surface, and when I did, gulping at air, I saw moonlight. I was only a couple of dozen yards away from both boats on the shoreward side. The machine gun chattered. Tracers knifed into the water five feet from my head, ricocheting and whining away. I surface-dived and stayed under and really swam.

That goddam moon was going to kill me. It was there again when I came up for air a second time. Their engine was throbbing. They were moving dead-slow to-

ward shore. They knew that was the way I had to go.
I heard the stitching and saw the tracers. They were too
high, over my head. I went under again.

The third time I surfaced I was almost a hundred
yards from them. The moon was playing hide-and-seek:
gone now. If I did a crawl or a butterfly I'd move faster,
but they might see me beating the water to froth. Still, I'd
make better time on the surface as long as there was no
moon. I settled for a sidestroke, with only my head out
of the water. I swam at an angle toward shore with
a couple of lights guiding me. They were heading
straight in as slow as they could run, idling and drifting every once in a while. They passed fifty yards alongside of me. And then the moon appeared.

I went under and kept swimming. Up again. The moon
was still there. They were closer to shore than I was,
and they must have realized they had gone too far too
fast. They began to circle. I treaded water, waiting for
my breathing to return to normal. Fatigue follows fear:
the body squandering its resources too quickly. I was
suddenly very tired.

They circled too far to the left and came slowly
around. I floated on my back. The moon disappeared behind a cloud again and I went into my sidestroke, only
my head above the surface, left arm thrust forward and
right arm thrust back and scissors kick and then bring
the left arm in and glide and start all over again. The
lights stayed where they were. I had a long way to go.
But the longer it took them to spot me, the less likely it
became that they would.

The moon was out again, and no clouds near it. I
treaded water and looked for them. They had returned
to MacPherson's boat. I swam on my back, sculling and
then doing an easy, back breast stroke and watching
them. After a long time the boats drifted apart. The
throb of their engine was faint. MacPherson's boat looked
wrong. It seemed lopsided. After a while aft and starboard it seemed to rise out of the water. The prow
went under. After that it sank quickly. The fishing boat
with its powerful engine headed east along the coast toward Torremolinos.

I swam shoreward, changing my stroke every few
minutes. A muscle bunched up in my left shoulder and

I had to turn over on my back and float. I was closer though. I could hear the gentle lapping of the surf. All of a sudden, without any doubt, I knew I would make it. And once I knew it, it was easy. It seemed only a few minutes after that when I dragged myself up on the beach. I couldn't stop panting and my knees were rubbery. The wind was cold. I stripped my sodden clothes off and sat down behind a rock on the beach, and then the wind wasn't so bad.

My head hit the sand. I stayed there. The rest of the world spun off into orbit.

chapter eleven

"Clever. Real clever," croaked a tired old voice like the cawing of the seagulls that had come to watch. "Mac-Pherson they had slated for death, and then you poked your proboscis in. Why not take care of both of us at once? You paid them two thousand bucks to have yourself killed."

I groaned and sat up. I felt as if I had run a three-minute mile—on my hands. Every muscle in my body was stiff and my throat hurt where the tough Spaniard had chopped at it with his fingers. My mouth was gritty and tasted like rotten fish. I gazed around. The gulls took off over the water. Outcroppings of rock, like the one I had slept behind, poked up from the sand of the beach. Behind me was a cliff like the one the Lancia had gone over. When was that, thirty-six hours ago? It didn't seem like more than six months.

A shadow moved over my face. I wasn't alone. The sun was low and the big shadow belonged to a small burro and two small boys shyly peering at me from the other side of the rock. They were up with the dawn collecting driftwood. The baskets hanging down the burro's scrawny flanks were almost full.

"Good morning," I said in a cheerful croak, and they retreated behind the rock again. I reached for my clothes. They were still wet. I spread them out on top of the rock, said, "Don't go away," and walked down the beach into the sea. I waded some and swam a little and returned dripping to the beach. The boys and their burro were still there. I found some change and sodden peseta notes in my trouser pocket. "Can you get me some coffee and something to eat?" I said. "Churros maybe?"

One of the boys nodded gravely. He didn't take the money, he just held out his hand for it. When I gave it to him the two boys and the burro paraded off down the beach toward Fuengirola.

I leaned against the rock, turning my face to the sun. Not only had the machine gun killed MacPherson, I thought, but first it had surprised the hell out of him. It wasn't the way the highjackers operated, but still he had recognized their boat. Which meant that their mission last night was not merely to lift his cargo but to kill him. He was armed, and Pez Espada hadn't liked that. Not only was he armed, but he had tried to talk the other contraband-runners into carrying weapons. Pez Espada had liked that even less.

Why? He sliced his one-third off the top of what Mac-Pherson and the other captains made, and he sold shares to pay for that part of their cargo they couldn't afford. He made a profit there too, charging whatever commission he would charge. But investing in smugglers' contraband was like investing in stocks—you could sink your money into Lunar Gold Mines, Inc. and watch it skyrocket to a fortune or watch it plunge off the bottom of the board, leaving you with certificates that might or might not make pretty wallpaper. The same with contraband. If highjackers lifted the cargo, you were clean out of luck. Not only wasn't there a profit, but there was a total loss. Better luck next time, pal.

But what if the highjackers took their orders from the broker? In this case, cigarettes. They'd sell for their ninety cents a pack and the profits would find their way back to Pez Espada or Manzanarez or whatever his name was, and there'd be no payoff to the investors. The cargo had been lost, hadn't it? Pez Espada would pocket the profits himself.

He couldn't do it too often, not unless he wanted to be called the unluckiest broker in Algeciras. If that happened, the investors would find themselves another middleman. But he could do it often enough to make a fortune, and he could get away with it if other highjackers, having nothing to do with Pez Espada, lifted other cargoes every now and then—which probably happeneo

But I wasn't interested in other highjackers. I was interested in Pez Espada. He had a nice game going, and MacPherson could have spoiled it, so MacPherson was murdered. I was poking around it and I had mentioned the Fuentes brothers and their cave, so I went on the same ride MacPherson went on. But half of Fuengirola knew the Fuentes brothers were smugglers. Then why all the fuss and bother?

I touched my shirt spread out on the rock. It wasn't dry, but it was dry enough. I got dressed, all but shoes. I didn't have any shoes. All the fuss and botther was because the Fuentes brothers weren't smugglers. They were highjackers—working with or for Pez Espada. And if it was assumed they were smugglers, that would be the best cover in the world. Everybody on the Costa del Sol loved a smuggler. Half of them invested their pesetas in contraband, through brokers like Pez Espada, and it was an easier way of turning a buck than taking a flyer on the loteria nacional. But highjackers they wouldn't love. Every time a cargo was lifted it was a total loss to the investors. Tough luck, chico. You can always ask about a consignment to Malta the next time you've scrapped together a few pesetas.

Had Robbie Hartshorn stumbled into that setup the way I had? If so, the Governor was wasting his money: by now Robbie Hartshorn would be a floater somewhere in the Mediterranean.

The boys and their burro came back along the beach. They had a jar full of hot coffee and half a dozen warm churros on a stick for me. I drank the coffee and ate four of the doughnut-like churros, giving the remaining two to the boys. Their burro mournfully watched us eat.

I traced a design in the sand with my bare toe. What I could do now was take my story to the Guardia, but how the hell would that help? Sergeant Martinez had warned me off. He was on the take. Whether he thought he was being paid by smugglers instead of highjackers was an interesting question, but letting him lift my passport for delivery at the border if I brought my story to him didn't seem the way to find out. Or could I wa until Maruja was sent to her cousin's place in Cari-

ʰuela, then see who or what turned up at the cave. But so
what? No doubt Pez Espada and his cronies would show
up, and we'd already met, thank you. Or I could go back
to the cave today and see the eighteen hundred cartons
of cigarettes for myself and maybe learn something or
other about the oddball relationship between Ruy Fuentes and Maruja. Tenley might or might not like what I
earned.

The trouble with all of that was it wouldn't necessari-
ly get me any closer to the mystery of Robbie Hartshorn's disappearance. Money or sex, I'd told his wife.
Looking for him, I'd messed with some of each. Either
way the trail always led back to the cave of Fuentes.
Unless I wanted to cable the Governor that except for
throwing away two thousand bucks of his money I'd
reached dead end, it looked like I'd have to pay another visit to the cave.

Hope for the best this time, I thought. Maybe this
time they won't greet you with a death-ride or an at-
tempted rape on the part of Maruja.

I walked barefoot along the beach into Fuengirola.
There was still the day to kill. If I hit the cave too early
I'd find Paco at home. If I waited until he headed for
the iron bull ring in late afternoon I might find the injured Ruy alone with Maruja.

Money or sex—or some of each? They are both what
make the planets spin, I thought, and yawned, and
stretched and turned to look far down the beach at the
tiny dots that were the two boys and their burro. The
way to kill the day, for someone who had spent the night
before as I had spent it, was to drag myself to a hotel
and crawl into a room and commune with Morpheus. I
was no growing child and didn't need eight hours of sleep
a night, but more than the hour and a half I'd had would
be nice.

I picked up a pair of rope sandals in a shop on a narrow street heading up from the beach to the caretera.
The farmacia next door supplied me with razor,
soap, toothbrush and paste. Other shops were just opening for business, their proprietors moving in that slow,
sleepy way Spaniards move in the early morning when

they know the day is going to be hot. They reminded me how bone-weary I was, as if I didn't already know it.

The hotel I found held down one corner of a square that had been strung with colored lightbulbs and crowded with stands and tents for the fair that followed the portable bull ring from small town to small town. A pair of Guardia were nosying around, and helped themselves to sardines that already had been grilled at one of the stands. A bootblack in his blue smock approached me, asked "Limpia botas?", saw my rope sandals, shrugged and went looking elsewhere.

I entered the hotel lobby, that was dark and cool and had a tile floor and a big stuffed bull's head over the clerk's desk. The head had been cleverly done. The bull's tongue protruded and it seemed to be frothing at the mouth.

"I'd like a room for today," I told the clerk.

"You mean now, this morning?" He was small and not at all dapper. He wore a dark blue jacket and no tie. His shirt collar was dirty, he needed a shave more than I did, the whites of his eyes were yellowish and red-flecked and he almost tripped over his shaking hand shoving a bottle of wine out of sight behind the desk.

"That's right," I said. "I'll be checking out late this afternoon. What I want is some sleep now."

He smiled. I smiled and waited while he looked me over. He said, "All the world has come to Fuengirola for the running of the bulls."

"I'm sure they have, but do you have a room?"

"The price," he said, still looking me over, "is three hundred pesetas—in advance for someone who wishes a room only by the day."

He kept drumming on the desk with his hand, over where he'd hid the bottle. I paid and he said, "If I may have your passport, señor?"

I'd forgotten that little detail about the passport. In Spain you don't just register at a hotel, you register through the hotel and by means of your passport with the police. For a moment I thought of Sergeant Martinez, but then I shrugged. By local standards Martinez was a bigshot: it would be several cuts beneath his dignity to fill out tourist cards. Some Guardia clerk as sleepy

as I was would scrawl a few words on a card, to show
I had spent the day in a hotel in Fuengirola, the card
would find its way, after normal Spanish delay, into a
musty file, and that would be that.

My passport was sodden. It was one of the old, paper-
covered green books, renewed, and the green dye had
run on the pages. The clerk handled it distastefully, swap-
ping a key on a metal plaque for it.

"No luggage?" he said.

"Not this trip."

"Conchita!" he called. "The maid will show you to
your room, señor."

She wore black, and a frilly white apron. Though her
mustache needed a bleach or a trim or both, she was
too young and too pretty to be wasting her time mop-
ping floors in a dive like this one—unless, as seemed likely by the way she wobbled her pelvis along the hall
ahead of me, she performed other functions, payment
naturally in advance, on request. She showed me to my
room, opened it with her own key, entered ahead of me,
pulled the cord that raised the shutters, turned and
smiled close to my face so I could get a whiff of the
garlic she'd eaten for breakfast, and asked, "You weesh
fleet?"

"Do I wish what?"

"Fleet." She made a spraying motion with her hands.
"For to keel flies. Fleet."

I told her no thanks, I wouldn't bother them if they
wouldn't bother me.

"You weesh anything else, you call for Concha. Anything, señor. Is why I am here. Americanos del Norte I
like. You un'erstan'?"

I said I understood. She went to the door reluctantly,
swishing her tail like a mare. I shut it behind her and
looked at the room. It contained an ancient brass bed
with what would be a lumpy mattress, a beat-up dresser
with a cracked glass top, a wooden chair and some hooks
on the wall instead of a closet. There was a chipped
sink in one corner, big enough to soak your head in if
you didn't have thick hair. I closed the shutters, having first looked out on the square with its tents and stands,
stripped off my rumpled clothes, crawled under the covers and fell asleep the way you shut off a light.

I lay on my right side, opened one eye a little and heard a band in the square playing *España Cani,* a patriotic song and a bullfighting song as Spanish as an authentic flamenco and almost as stirring. They had a pretty sweet trumpet down there. I listened contentedly, telling myself it was the music that had awakened me, until I smelled the garlic.

There was a sigh next to me on the lumpy mattress as I rolled over on my back. The garlic smell grew strong enough to scare off the Evil Eye. Hair tickled my cheek. Something soft and firm at the same time, which only could have been a woman's breast, brushed against my left arm.

"Querido," smiled Concha, "I thought you would sleep, and sleep, and sleep."

I sat up. She tugged at my arm, but not very hard. "Scram," I said. "I told you I understand. I didn't say I was interested."

"No comprendo," she said in a husky voice. She tried to draw me down. Beyond her on the back of the room's single chair I saw her black dress and the frilly white apron and nothing else. Concha was a girl who could get ready to perform her services, if you wanted them, in jig-time.

"Dress yourself," I told her in Spanish, "and go mop some floors. I came here to sleep."

"Truly, Querido? You do not mean that."

She glanced at the door—too anxiously. I was suddenly wide awake. I got up fast, grabbing her elbow and yanking her off the bed. She was as naked as the truth every detective hopes to find. Again she glanced at the door, nervously.

"Get going, sister," I said. "With or without your dress. It's all the same to me. What I ought to do is throw you out the window."

Her smooth shoulders slumped. She looked crestfallen and contrite. "I make beeg mistake. If you weesh it, I go."

She went to the chair and picked up her dress. But instead of slipping into it, she grasped it firmly with both hands and ripped it from collar to hem. Then, while I stood there in my shorts gaping, she let go with a scream. It would have done a howler monkey, that can be heard for five miles, proud.

There was a sound at the door, as of a key being inserted in the lock. Concha, still naked, her face still in repose as it had remained during the scream, hurled herself at me. She screamed again, breathed garlic at me and clawed my face with the sharp nails of her left hand.

That was when the door opened.

The small, dirty-collared and yellow-eyed clerk had been waiting in the wings with Sergeant Martinez. On cue they entered. Concha flung herself on the bed, sobbing. The clerk was drunk. Sergeant Martinez removed his winged patent-leather hat, gave me a wistful smile and then a reproachful scowl.

Concha, sobbing, recited, "This man called me, to prepare a bath he said. I came along the hall. The door was open. I entered. He shut the door. He was not dressed, except as you see him. He attacked me. I screamed."

"Fortunately for you," I said, "Sergeant Martinez happened to be right outside in the hall."

Sergeant Martinez said, "Conchita, compose yourself and repeat what you have said."

She repeated it, word for word, while Sergeant Martinez smiled his wistful smile at me again. We both knew, of course, he would get away with it. There wasn't any doubt. There never is, in Spain, not if the Guardia Civil decides to lean on you.

The repetition of Concha's speech, without sobs, was to give the clerk the cue he'd failed to pick up. He was staring drunkenly and lecherously at Concha's bare plump posterior.

"Señor Lorca," Martinez asked, "she is a good girl?"

On cue this time, Lorca said, "Other chambermaids I have known would perhaps, for money . . . . accommodate a rich American . . . . but never Conchita, the daughter of my sister-in-law's cousin."

"Then if she says he attacked her, you believe this?"

"Clearly," Lorca agreed. He couldn't get his eyes off Concha. "It is a thing I am sure of."

"Then you would make an official denunciation of this man?"

"Since he tried to attack the daughter of my sister-in-law's cousins, it is my duty."

"And you, pobrecita?" Martinez asked Concha.

The poor little thing sniffled, "If it is my duty."

It was her duty. Lorca brought her a new dress, and she put it on. I got dressed.

Two more Guardia were in the hall. We all went outside and through the square, that was crowded now in mid-afternoon. I was flanked by the two Guardia. In badly wrinkled shirt and slacks and needing a shave, I must have looked sinister. Every pair of eyes turned to watch our little procession as it left the square, went along the street to the Guardia substation and up the stairs there and under the sign that said: *Toda por la Patria.*

chapter twelve

I never laid eyes on the official denunciations made by Sr. Lorca and Concha, but they must have been beauties. If a foreigner is denounced in Spain, and it happens to some of the cut-ups among the expatriate set on the Costa del Sol, he is usually granted a couple of weeks to clear out. I wasn't given any time at all.

Back I went into the small whitewashed room. Through its thick door as the afternoon became evening I heard voices and comings and goings and the ringing of a telephone and a hunt-and-peck typist at work. Somewhere along in there Sr. Lorca's voice and Concha's went away, and other voices, male, took their place. I heard laughter too, but it wasn't very encouraging.

At seven the street was crowded with aficionados leaving the iron bull ring—an occasional loud voice quickly swallowed by the shuffle of many feet. You are subdued and in no mood to talk when you have seen the running of the bulls.

By eight the fiesta in the square had started up again. There was music and singing and shouting and fireworks. The main room of the Guardia substation had become quiet. Just when I decided they had forgotten all about me, the lock turned and the door opened and Don Quixote minus his beard smiled in at me.

"We have your reservations," he said.

"Where am I going?"

"Where do you think?"

"Well, not to the Alcazar, I guess."

He laughed. He could afford to. His side had won. Why get into a stew?

"Iberia Airlines from Malaga to Madrid at ten-forty. The two o'clock Air France flight from Madrid to Paris. What you do after reaching Paris is your own affair."

"As long as what I do doesn't get done in Spain."

"You are finished in Spain."

"I guess I shouldn't complain," I said. "Being kicked out isn't so bad. It's better than what happened to Stu Huntington. It's better than what happened to an American contraband-runner named MacPherson. They shot him inside the three-mile limit, by the way. He was murdered in Spain. Naturally you don't know what I'm talking about."

"Naturally."

"Naturally you never heard of anyone named Pez Espada."

"It is as you say."

"Or Señor Manzanarez?"

He shrugged. Looking at him, I thought both names had meant nothing to him. He seemed puzzled.

"Would I have banged my head against a brick wall if I hadn't been denounced, sergeant? Is Robbie Hartshorn dead?"

"I wish, señor, somebody could inform me. It is my job to find him."

"Sure. It's also your job, as you see it, to take your cut from smugglers who run their contraband up the coast from Gibraltar."

"Señor," Martinez asked with reproachful erudition, "don't you know the story of El Cid, the national hero of Spain, who stole from the rich to give to the poor?"

"A Spanish Robin Hood. Uh-huh. So what?"

"Suppose the little people along this coast could profit from the activities of these smugglers, by investing in small percentages of their cargo in advance. It is such a terrible thing that is being done?" Martinez smiled his Don Quixote smile. "Of course, if you repeat what I have said to anyone, I would deny it. But suppose, just suppose, the poor are made a little less poor by this smuggling. Suppose it means milk for a sick child or meat on the family table once a week. Suppose it means a doctor's fee when a doctor can make the difference between life and death. Suppose—"

"Suppose," I cut him off, "you weren't dealing with smugglers who bought their cargo in Gibraltar, part of which the little people you were talking about invested in. Suppose you were dealing with highjackers. Suppose you'd been duped, sergeant."

"Highjackers? I do not understand the word."

I explained. "They lift the cargo from the smugglers, sergeant. Having made no investment at all, they sell it in Spain. And since it was a total loss to the runners of contraband, it's a total loss to the small investors. No milk, no meat, no doctors, no difference between life and death. Suppose that's what the Fuentes brothers have been doing, right under your nose?"

He started to smile again, but took a look at my face and changed his mind. He made clubs of his hands and raised them toward his face and stared at them. He said softly, "You're mad."

"You could check on a bodega in Algeciras called *La Perla*. It's run by a guy named Manzanarez and known, to a few people, as Pez Espada. He's a contraband broker. He knows which cargoes are worth lifting and which aren't. He knows how often he can get away with it. Suppose he passes the word along to the Fuentes brothers who, let's say, own a fast cruiser disguised as a fishing boat. They use it to lift the smugglers' cargo. Your little people never have a chance."

Martinez began to relax. "The Fuentes brothers own no such craft. If, in fact, anyone in Fuengirola did, I would know of it. Fuengirola is only a village, señor."

"Torremolinos is bigger, and close. That's where the highjackers' boat was heading last night. They've got dozens of fishing boats pulled up on the beach at Carihuela." An idea hit me then, and I went on, "Doña Maruja has a cousin in Carihuela, doesn't she? Maybe they're keeping it in the family. Maybe the boat belongs to him."

"I still say you are mad. Why should I believe what you tell me?"

"Why don't you look into it? I can't—now."

For a while Martinez said nothing. He sat on the bare

bedspring and stared between his knees at the floor.
"What they have been doing is no evil thing," he said at
last. "I have not been dishonoring my uniform to turn
away and let them do it. Mother of God, man, I've
known Ruy Fuentes all his life, and his father before
him. Ruy is a good boy. He would not do such a thing
as you suggest."

"Was it his idea to send Concha to my room at the
hotel?"

"Your passport. It came with some others. It was wet.
The duty non-com was puzzled, and brought it to my
attention. I called Doña Maruja, and she said you had been
to the cave again. I did what I had to do."

"Sure. Was covering up Stu Huntington's murder
something you had to do?"

That was the right question from my point of view but
the wrong one from his. He clammed up on me. He
took a pack of Bisontes from the pocket of his uniform
blouse and lit one. He tossed the pack at me. I had a
smoke. A few minutes later one of the Guardia poked
his head in through the doorway to say, "El coche,
sargente. Está aquí."

"The car for the airport," Martinez told me, and we
went outside together into the noise of the fiesta.

Malaga Airport shared a pattern of runways with the
military airbase on the coastal littoral midway between
Torremolinos and Malaga. The terminal building was low
and rambling, its tile roof and restaurant patio lit by
floodlights, its observation deck lit by baby-spots.

We drove through the gate in the high cyclone and
barbed wire fence about an hour before flight time. For
company I had the two Guardia who had escorted me
from the hotel. The older one looked bored and indifferent. The younger looked very satisfied with himself.
I decided he was the one who would accompany me
on the flight to Madrid to see that I boarded the Air
France plane. It wasn't every day a provincial cop
got as far as the capital.

If this had been anywhere but Spain the rest of what
happened wouldn't have happened. The older cop or his
young sidekick would have produced a pair of nippers,
I'd have been handcuffed to one of them on the ride
and handcuffed to the one who went with me to Ma-

drid, and that would have been that. But this was Spain, and while tourism may have been a fun thing for the Americans toting their cameras and Fielding's Travel Guides in and out of the airport, it was serious business to the boys who had to balance the Spanish budget. Anything that smacked of a police state, especially as it applied to an American, even if a rumpled and beard-sprouting American, would be as welcome as a black-widow spider in a love nest.

So look, ma, I started thinking as the car pulled up near the baggage platform and we got out, no handcuffs. It was just an idea, but as such ideas will, it nibbled. We entered the terminal building through a side door and past a creaky guard who looked old enough to have earned his sinecure as a veteran of the Spanish American War. He wore high leather boots, crossed leather bandoliers on his gray uniform blouse and a high-crowned sombrero with the brim rolled and the chin strap secured under his wattles. At his side was a holster that might have been stuffed with cobwebs. He saluted the Guardia, and they saluted him. He gave me a gravely bored look, as if every night two or three deportees passed through the door he guarded. Maybe they did.

Inside, a uniformed dispatcher who seemed to be expecting us gave the older Guardia some forms to fill out. The younger one motioned me to a bench along one wall of the small room and sat down next to me. The minute hand on a wall-clock jerked forward two minutes, as if it had been asleep on the job and suddenly remembered what it was supposed to do. From an amplifier on the wall a woman's voice blared the arrival of an Iberian Airlines flight from Barcelona, and pretty soon I could hear the plane's engines as it taxied up outside. The minute hand of the clock jerked again, kicking into the past two minutes of the time Governor Hartshorn was paying me for.

I began to feel frustrated and angry. What I have to sell is time, whatever brains I come equipped with, and enough guts to do what has to be done in a world neither the Governor nor I had made. Time was passing, whatever brains I own had been enough to uncover the high-jacking setup but not enough to learn what had happened to Robbie Hartshorn, and my intestinal fortitude, such as it was, hadn't earned me a thing this trip. Now I was being thrown out of Spain, and if I caught the first jet from Paris to New York and the first plane from New York to Washington, tomorrow I could be sipping mint juleps with the Governor and telling him, sorry old boy but it looks as if we don't get to find out what happened to your son. Well, the hell with him. He was a drunkard anyway.

The minute hand jerked again. The Guardia finished filling out his papers. A dark and pretty ground hostess came in, and he stood against the wall staring at her speculatively and scratching his belly.

Look, ma, I thought again, no handcuffs. But both Guardia wore pistol holsters, and theirs wouldn't be stuffed with cobwebs.

At ten-fifteen the dispatcher spoke to the older Guardia, who looked at me and nodded. The young Guardia stood up. I got after him and he took my arm in a grip as easy to break as the news I would have to break to Governor Hartshorn.

We all went through another door to a gravel path skirting the dining patio on the tarmac side of the terminal building. A crowd of tourists were milling behind a chain to our left, as tourists do when they are waiting for a plane on which the seats haven't been assigned. When we passed them I heard voices speaking English.

"Why don't they let us board?" a woman asked her husband querulously. "That's our plane out there, the Viscount."

"It's still early," he said.

"But if it's our plane. Look at this mob! There won't be enough seats to go around. I've heard how they sometimes over-book, and then you're just out of luck if you.
—"

"It's still early," the man said. He was embarrassed.

"Well, when they let that chain down you just grab my hand and run. Hear, Hector?"

"Okay, okay already," Hector said.

We passed them. The woman said, *"They're* boarding now."

"They're police," Hector said.

"Does that make their tickets any better than ours?"

"Please, dear," Hector said.

I heard a clanking sound. Hector's wife had unhooked

the chain from its stanchion and dropped the loose end on the concrete apron bordering the gravel path.

"Eloise," Hector said.

Footsteps crunched on gravel behind us.

What the Guardia had intended avoiding by getting me aboard early was the walking race that develops when a planeload of anxious tourists are told their flight is ready. I'd seen it happen at a dozen airports: a ground hostess usually leads them out, setting a brisk but dignified pace. But then the tourists, thinking of window seats in any plane, thinking of forward seats in a pure jet and aft seats in a jet-prop like the Viscount, really start stepping out. And when they do, the ground hostess would have to be a Wilma Rudolph to keep up with them.

It was happening now. Eloise and her reluctant husband overtook us. A spry old number carrying a raincoat slung over one arm overtook us. A young couple half-trotting hand in hand overtook us. By the time we had covered half the distance to the Viscount, we were caught up in the walking race.

A pair of floodlights from the roof of the terminal building gleamed on the Viscount's sleek silver skin. There were lights on poles at the edge of the patio behind us, but it was quite dark on what now had become a race-course and pitch dark to right and left. Darkness, and passengers walking hard on their heels, not quite running. The Guardia couldn't go for their guns, not unless their lives depended on it. Robbie Hartshorn's life, if Robbie Hartshorn was still alive, might depend on my getting away from them.

The younger Guardia was still holding my arm. Two fat German women in tweedy suits too hot for the climate stomped by. I started walking faster, as if the race was contagious. The Guardia didn't like that. If we couldn't board first they wanted us to board last, after the game of musical chairs inside the Viscount. The one holding my arm yanked back on it. I helped out by stopping suddenly and driving my elbow into his middle. He squawed and bent and let go of my arm. I sprinted off as fast as I could into the darkness, doubling back toward the far end of the terminal building. That was the most direct route to the gate. They'd know I had to head for it. It was the only way out. I had to beat them there.

I hit the asphalt road beyond the terminal, my knees still driving hard. Ahead I could see the light over the gate. Seventy-five yards, maybe a hundred. Just a few seconds, but this was the bad place. I'd be silhouetted against the light. If they felt in the mood for plinking at fugitive deportees, they might take some pot shots at me. Maybe Sergeant Martinez would pin a medal on them.

With fifty yards to go, I ran off the road and across a lawn and through some hedges. I hunkered down behind the hedges, getting my breath. In a few seconds one of the Guardia came running past, and then the other. The second one ran at a crouch and had lost his hat. Both had their guns drawn. They rushed out through the gate. I heard footsteps pounding pavement, and then silence. What would I do in their place? I'd split up, one heading for Torremolinos, one for Malaga. There were only two. There wasn't a third who could cross the road and search along the beach. Or, even if they decided on the beach instead of the road, which wasn't likely because they knew a fugitive would make better time on pavement and might even get a lift, I could hug the shadows near the cliffs looming over the sand and still make it safely to Torremolinos.

I trotted up to the gate and waited there a while. Maybe they figured I might let them pass me. Maybe one of them was lurking in wait out there. Beyond the cone of light I could see nothing. I stooped for a handful of gravel from the road-shoulder and tossed it through the gate. No response. I slipped out fast, crossed the road and a field that was furrowed and under cultivation and a screen of high rushes to break the sea wind, and then I was on the beach. A half-mile to my right, the cliffs began.

It was four miles or better to Torremolinos. I started walking.

chapter thirteen

Midnight had come and gone by the time I climbed the stairs to the high terrace of La Atalaya, the Hartshorn villa. Nothing had changed, not even the inevitable expatriate party. Flamenco music wailed from hi-fi, every window except those in the bedroom wing was brightly lit and a woman even drifted out on the terrace when I arrived.

This time I was lugging the memory of two hard nights instead of my B-4 bag, and this time I was winded. The woman wasn't Nancy Huntington. This one was a studious-looking and not particularly sober blonde with frizzly hair.

"I needed some air," she told me. "Lordie-lord-lord, the way some people never stop yammering. Needed some air too, I'll bet. Huh?"

"What I need they put out in bottles. Is Tenley around?"

"If so, she wouldn't be in that auditorium they call a living room. She Hates the Expatriate Set—all with capital letters, please. Might be reading in her own room or downstairs talking with the maids, those who aren't making up snacks as fast as those hungry mouths in there can gobble them."

"Which one would be Tenley's room?"

The frizzly-haired blonde said, "Did anybody ever tell you you had a sexy voice? You do, you know."

I said nothing. Idly I wondered how she'd made up her mind about that, since she'd done most of the talking. "I've got a theory about voices," she said. "You can always tell how sexy a man is going to be by his voice. Take actors now. Louis Hayward, there was a bird who couldn't act for beans in my book, but he had one helluva sexy voice. Or Orson Welles. I met Orson on the Riviera a few seasons back at Gabrielle Reynaud's villa on the Cap. Your voice reminds me of—"

A small, scrawny man with a bitter mouth stood by the open French doors at the end of the terrace. "There you are," he said, "and running off at the mouth as usual about those sexy voices of yours. Amigo, did she tell you you had a sexy voice? A real sexy voice maybe like Orson Welles?" He told the blonde bitterly, "You try climbing into bed on a cold night with a sexy voice."

"Ah, Charlie," she said.

"Shut up and come on inside where I can keep an eye on your sexy ears. Though why the hell I bother, that I don't know."

"Ah, Charlie," she said again.

"Shut up."

"What did I do? What did I say? I just—"

They went inside whining at each other.

I found Tenley in the large kitchen with a couple of old Spanish women in black dresses and white aprons making fancy little sandwiches, the kind you eat at one fast nibble and then wonder what they were and then say the hell with it and take a drink. Tenley was wearing tapered slacks and a red blouse with a scoop-neckline. The smile she gave me when I came in was worth flying three thousand miles for.

"Am I glad to see you," she said. "When I woke up and found your note, I started imagining all sorts of things— none of them good." She flushed then, remembering our last moments together. "Did you. . . . did we. . . . do anything?"

"Don't you know?"

"I guess it runs in the family. I was looped."

"I was noble," I said. "I tucked you in, that's all."

She looked relieved, but a little wistful too. "You're a nice guy, Chet."

"I'm a fugitive," I said, and then told her what had happened. She listened with mounting impatience, as if she had something to say and wished I'd finished so she could spit it out. "Next time," I told her, "they'll probably put the nippers on me and deliver me to the border in a sealed van. Is there a gun in this house? Did your father have one?"

"As a matter of fact, he did. Not that he ever used it. It was a Beretta he took off an Italian officer during the war. He was very proud of it. What do you want a gun for?"

"I'm going back to the cave. Why does anybody want a gun?"

"She's not at the cave," Tenley said quickly.

"Who? Maruja?"

"She came here about an hour ago."

That surprised me. "Maruja was here?" I asked stupidly. "You mean at La Atalaya?"

"That's right. She came looking for Fernando Robles. They went off together."

The blind sculptor and the gypsy woman, I thought, getting no message out of it. Then Tenley said, "I intended following them, but a noisy drunk cornered me on the terrace and began chewing my ear off. By the time I reached the bottom of the stairs, they were gone. What would Maruja be doing in Torremolinos, Chet? The way I heard it, she never left the cave."

"Sometimes she did. She's got a cousin who lives in Carihuela. The highjacking boat could be his."

"I'll never believe Ruy had anything to do with high-jacking—or murder."

"You been back to Fuengirola? How is he?"

She looked away. "I don't know. I wanted to see him. I got cold feet. I couldn't face him and Maruja, not after the last time I saw them together. What are you going to do?"

"Borrow your old man's gun if I can, then go looking for Maruja's cousin."

"You're like a bulldog," she sighed. "Sometimes I wish you'd never come to Spain. Sometimes I'm afraid of what you're going to find."

"Anything specific in mind?"

She shook her head. "No. I'm so confused. Ruy would never . . . . he's so gentle . . . . he's no criminal. Wait here. I'll get the gun."

While she was getting it, I popped a dozen of the tiny sandwiches in my mouth. A few minutes later, with the Beretta in my belt and my shirttails out, I was heading down the outside stairs. Tenley called after me soft-ly, "Chet? About the gun?"

I waited. "My father always said it would make a— a fitting suicide weapon. He'd had to kill the Italian of-ficer, you see. It was the only time he saw action in the war. When he was drunk he often said he felt like a murderer. Sometimes he used to fondle the gun, almost lovingly, and Andrea had to take it away from him. It would be fitting, he said, almost as if the Italian, his victim, came back to murder him. He used to say that's why he took to drinking."

It wasn't enough reason. It never is. I started thinking of a command post near the Elbe River, and a white-blond kid in Hitler's final desperate army who couldn't have been more than sixteen. I hadn't been exactly a graybeard. I'd had four years on him. He'd loomed out of the night, firing once, getting my left arm above the elbow. I let him have my bayonet in the chest and I had to plant my combat boot against his ribs and lean all my weight on it to get the blade gratingly out. There were fifty million of us, I thought, in every country's uniform, and some of us got killed and most of us did the killing. It wasn't enough reason. It never is.

Midway on the beach between Torremolinos and Montemar, a smaller more exclusive watering-place for the expatriate set, the little whitewashed houses of Carihuela huddled on their narrow, crooked streets. It was still just a fishing village, a stubborn anachronism whose every street seemed to end on the water, bordered on one side by high cliffs and on the other by a steel-and-glass hotel that was the last word in Miami Beach modern, complete with tile tennis courts, a spotlit swimming pool and a doorman in white livery who could direct the Caddies and Mercedes Benzes around the big circular driveway in fourteen languages.

I hit the beach at the cliff end of Carihuela. A fat Mediterranean moon greeted me, and the winking eyes of the lights of a string of fishing boats about half a mile offshore. At the far end of the beach, the tall tower of the luxury hotel, all lit up, looked like an electronic phallic symbol. A few of the ungainly boats weren't out that night. They'd been drawn up on the sand on wooden runways, and fishermen sat under their prows near small olive-wood fires, mending nets. Spain is nothing if not stylized: every boat, every fisherman, every net stretched on the sand, every fire on the beach looked the same.

The first five fishermen never heard of Maruja. Their responses were stylized too. They looked at me, then glanced over their shoulders at the big hotel, assuming I had come from it and wondering what had brought me out of its sterile twentieth century world to a beach eroded by sewage ditches and backed by shanties where in the darkness pigs snuffled in the garbage heaps for their middle of the night snacks and where, lit by an occasional fire, the fishermen worked the night through because they preferred darkness to the heat of the day.

The sixth fisherman, more than halfway across the beach, gave me the same no answer. He was sitting crosslegged with a teen-aged boy, both of them mending a net. "No, señor," the man said. "Never have I heard of this gypsy Maruja." He waited gravely for me to go away, not impatient and not unfriendly, but as closed as a clam. But the boy looked at me with interest.

"Many gypsies live in Carihuela," he said. "Many others visit here."

"Enough, chico," grumbled the man, and then I knew I was getting the silent treatment from all of them. If they knew Maruja and Maruja's cousin, and in a place as small as Carihuela probably they did, why should they tell me? A foreigner in the middle of the night, who came snooping around for no reason they could see?

I stood there, waiting. The boy kept looking at me. The man shrugged and picked up a wineskin, holding it out at arm's length and squirting a hissing stream of wine into the back of his throat before biting off the stream and dropping the skin. It looks easy but isn't. You need plenty of practice before you can do it without squirting wine all over your face. I'd had the practice, long ago, with a girl I knew in Washington whose father had been the American consul in Barcelona. She used to pass a wineskin around at parties and squeal with delight at all the wine on all the surprised faces. My eventual facility with it had led to pleasanter things, as if that was the way she tested her men. Who needs a sexy voice?

I wondered if I remembered the technique. It seems easy until you have had enough, and then, when you try to stop the flow of wine, that's when it gets sloppy.

"My throat is dry as the sand," I said gravely in Spanish.

A looked passed between the man and the boy. Spaniards are hospitable, but they're not above having a laugh at the expense of a foreigner. "Forgive me, señor," said the man. He passed the wineskin to me and waited expectantly. The boy smiled a little in anticipation.

I raised the skin, titlted the nozzle down toward my face, parted my lips and squeezed. The wine, acid but earthy, jetted into my throat. I held the stream, steady and hissing, a few seconds more than the fisherman had. Then I bit it off cleanly, turned the skin up and returned it gravely to its owner. "Gracias, señor," I said. "Your wine is excellent."

"I thank you for saying so. It is from the vines of my uncle who lives in Churriana."

"Commend him for me."

"As you say, señor." He smiled a grave Spanish smile. He was pleased with the way I had handled the skin.

"Adiós."

"Adiós."

I started walking off, in no hurry.

"Señor? A moment. Is this not the best of all ways to drink the good vino tinto?"

"If the wine's good, any way's good to drink it."

"Who was it you said you wished to find?"

"A gypsy woman called Maruja, who lives in Fuengirola. Or her cousin who lives here in Carihuela."

"It has just returned to my memory, señor. A man, a fisherman in the village, has a cousin who is a gypsy from Fuengirola. He is called Rafael Jímenez."

"Rafael Jímenez, that is right," the boy said.

They told me how to find Rafael Jímenez's house. I left the beach with a silent thanks for the American consul's daughter.

chapter fourteen

The houses were connected, their doorways opening on the unpaved street with no intermediary sidewalk or stoops. Most of the doorways were blocked by nothing more substantial than heavy hanging curtains, and the continuous wall of adobe façade was white as bone in the moonlight. Distantly I heard the metallic tears of a flamenco guitar sobbing its tragic song into the night.

Then I heard brisk footsteps. I drifted into the shadow of a curtained doorway, waiting, remembering I was a fugitive, holding my breath. A Guardia came by in his winged patent-leather hat, confident and cocky. That was all I needed. They probably had my description by now all down the coast from Malaga to Algeciras. The Guardia stalked up the street, a sten gun slung on his shoulder. I waited, and didn't quite jump a foot when a man called out in his sleep on the other side of the curtained doorway.

Rafael Jímenez's house was the fourth from the corner, this street. When I reached it, the guitar was fainter.

The doorway was curtained. Beyond the heavy hanging I heard voices, a man's choked with anger, a woman's placating but caustic. They were speaking Spanish.

"I'm telling you that is too much money," the man said. "Where is my profit? I take risks too."

"We all take risks, Fernando," the woman said, and I recognized the throaty purr of the gypsy Maruja. "I take risks, my cousin Rafael takes risks, my boys do. We all take risks. And you have been telling me the same thing for an hour."

"Was it for this Huntington was killed?"

"You know why Huntington was killed."

"I know that now, after he is dead, you ask too much money."

"It is not my idea, but his. The new one."

"Then tell him I won't pay. I refuse to pay that much."

"Very well. Then you don't get them."

There was a silence. Fernando said, "Take me back."

"Very well," Maruja said again, indifferently.

"No. Wait. This one time I will pay what he demands. But only this one time."

"That," Maruja said, "is between the two of you."

"I will see him," Fernando said threateningly.

Maruja laughed. "Then see him. Argue with him. Don't argue with me."

"In the morning I'm going to Ronda."

"He won't like that."

"I don't like what I have to pay. Take me back."

"To La Atalaya?"

"No. My house."

"The money first."

I heard a chair scrape back, then footsteps beyond the curtain. I moved silently to the next doorway and flattened myself in its darkness.

A few seconds later Maruja and Fernando came out. His hand rested lightly on her arm. They started walking. I didn't have to follow them. I knew where they were going. I gave them five minutes and made my way through the narrow Carihuela streets to the highway and along that back to Torremolinos and down the Calle San Miguel, that nobody called the Avenida Generalísimo Franco though officially that was its name, and down the steps at the end of the street to the sculptor's house.

No sounds there, except the faint rustling of the night wind in the rushes back of the house. I waited a few yards off in the darkness, wishing I had a cigarette and wondering if Maruja had come and gone, wondering if North Country would be home from the shindig at La Atalaya yet, and if home, sleeping.

Then I heard a clinking sound from the back of the house, steady, rhythmic, not very loud. I gave Maruja another five minutes, but she didn't show up. If she'd returned up the steps, I'd have passed her, but she could have gone back to her cousin's place in Carihuela along the beach. I decided to do some more snooping.

What I forgot was that the object of my snooping was a blind man. The back of the house, facing away from the moonlight, was dark. I could barely make out two windows on ground level. The steady *clink-clink-clink* came from one of them. Fernando could have been hard at work on a bronze to turn Rodin's ghost green with envy, but he was a blind man and he wouldn't need any light to do it.

Thirty minutes dragged themselves by like weary and blindfolded picadors' nags, battered and scarred and wishing they were on the way to the glue factory instead of waiting for the sound of the bull's hooves and the feel of its horns. Along the beach, a dog yipped. All of a sudden the clinking sound stopped. The shutters of the window opened then and Fernando's head appeared there. I was all of two feet from him. He leaned on the sill, took a few deep breaths of the sea air, yawned, stretched, seemed to stare straight at me, yawned again, ducked his head back and pulled the shutters in after him. Then I heard footsteps in the house, receding. That would mean Fernando was going to bed.

His hearing would be good, probably much more acute than mine. I remained where I was, giving him time to fall asleep. Another fifteen minutes left the future, lingered a long minute at a time in the present, and became the past.

I tugged at the shutters. They weren't fastened. I climbed in over the sill and stood still. My eyes were as accustomed to the dark as they were going to get. I could see nothing, and I hadn't come equipped with a box of matches. Slowly I groped my way around the room. My legs struck a table. I fingered its surface: a wooden mallet first, and then twelve statuettes, their metal skins cool, their legs upright on pedestals that felt like wood. I ran my fingers over them. They seemed to be figurines about a foot high. From their stance and the way their metal arms were extending to one side and the tiny sheets of metal dropping from those arms, I decided they were little bronze bullfighters. Who was it that had told me Fernando was a sculptor who knew his stuff? Andrea Hartshorn, I remembered, that first night. But what he had been working on, if my fingertips weren't deceiving me, were tritely stylized figurines of bullfighters for the tourist trade.

I decided to take one of them out the window with me and find some light to examine it by. I picked one up. Something scraped at the window and the shutters, which I had pulled closed, opened into the night. I crouched near the table. I wasn't the only one snooping in Fernando's studio.

The room was so dark that I couldn't see the new intruder, except as more substantial blackness. But I could smell her, and there was no mistaking Maruja's musky perfume. She'd been waiting outside, way off in the rushes probably, until Fernando was finished for the night. Had she seen me? No—otherwise she wouldn't have made like a second-story man. I crouched there without moving. She came unerringly to the table, as if she could see in darkness like a cat. One of her legs brushed my shoulder lightly. It meant nothing to her; I was part of the furniture. Suddenly a match flared. I tensed. If she saw me then, and in a second she would, she might cry out. I stood up quickly behind her and cupped a hand over her mouth. She struggled against me, writhing. It was hard to hold her. She made a mewling sound, and I clamped my hand harder across her mouth.

"They'll hear us," I whispered in Spanish against her ear. "Don't struggle, Maruja. All I want is information. I won't hurt you. Can I let go?"

She nodded her head. When I released her, she struck another match. "You," she said.

"Uh-huh. Looking for the same thing you're looking for." I didn't add: only you know what it is, and I don't. By the light of the match I could see I was right about

Fernando's work—bronze bullfighters that might fetch five bucks a piece on the tourist market, if the tourists weren't very discerning.

The match went out. I said, "First you sell the stuff to him, then you come here to steal it back. You do that often?"

She laughed softly, deep in her throat. "Never before. Why should I have done so before?"

I took a stab, "Because he's going to Ronda tomorrow?"

"He's finished if he does. And if he is finished, he won't need these." By these she meant the statues. I felt myself scowling in the darkness. The statues were small, but not that small. Even between them, Fernando and Maruja couldn't have carried a dozen of the figurines back from Carihuela. Besides, this was Fernando's studio. This was where he did the work. And there had been that clinking sound. Half an hour of it. Enough time for what?

I picked up one of the figurines. It was light. Fernando, his wife had told me, worked in lost wax. The figurines would be hollow then. Half an hour would have been more than enough time for him to attach them to their bases. With what inside?

"If you pull, it comes apart," Maruja said. "You don't know what is inside, do you? You don't know, eh señor?" She struck another match. "Then look if you must."

I held the figurine in one hand and its wooden base in the other. I gave a yank, and they separated. The legs of the statue were close together, a single bronze unit in the close-step of a pasa doble. I poked a finger up their hollowness and felt a strip of tape inside the knees. Three small hard lumps were under the tape. I got a fingernail under its edge and pulled it off and then withdrew it. Maruja lit another match while I turned the tape sticky side up.

The facets of three small diamonds reflected the light of the match up at me.

About a carat each, I decided. Nothing to make the owner of the Hope Diamond wish he could swap, but they looked well cut and if they were flawless they'd probably fetch close to a grand a piece. If each statue contained three of them, that meant there was thirty-six thousand bucks worth of diamonds on Fernando's work table. If they'd come off MacPherson's boat then the murdered smuggler had been holding out on me. His cargo like hell had been only cigarettes, not that you could sneeze at cigarettes at Spain's black market prices.

"And now?" Maruja asked me.

"He wants to see who in Ronda?"

She didn't answer.

"Pez Espada?"

"Seguro," she nodded. "Pez Espada."

I remembered the tough little Spaniard, Diego, and his fat sidekick, Estebán. "I wish him luck."

"He will need it. Mucho suerte, the great fool. What are you going to do?"

I thought of the two thousand bucks, Governor Hartshorn's money, Pez Espada had taken off me as an investment in MacPherson's doomed cargo. I slipped the tape and its three diamonds in my pocket. "Pez Espada owes me that," I said.

"It is all you wish?"

It was all I wished. Quickly in the darkness, Maruja separated the other figurines from their bases and unfastened the tapes. She went to the window before I did. When she climbed through I followed her. She waited for me, politely. She was in no hurry to get away. She turned left away from the beach, toward the steel ramp and steps leading up to the Calle San Miguel that was called the Avenida Generalísimo Franco only officially.

The ramp circled, climbing. At first the steps were a dozen feet apart, and then six, and then three. On one side of us were the blank façades of houses like those in Carihuela, on the other a stone wall no more than a yard high and beyond it a long drop down to the lower levels of the ramp.

We had ascended side by side about halfway to the mill tower that gives Torremolinos its name when Maruja said, softly and almost pleasantly, "Paco. Kill him."

I whirled, peering into the darkness, feeling my spine crawl when I remembered the hold Maruja had on the Fuentes brothers and the size and strength of the picador Paco. If she told him to kill me, he'd go about it the same way he went about sticking el toro with his stopped pick.

Nothing at first. I reached for Robbie Hartshorn's gun,

then changed my mind. As a bluff it would get me nothing in the darkness, and I couldn't use it. One shot and the Guardia, who patroled the beach and the streets of Torremolinos all night, would come running. The next thing I knew, I'd be in Madrid en route home with three diamonds for the Governor but no answers and no missing son.

All that went through my mind in a split second, while I was looking for Paco. Then Maruja moved away from me, and then I saw his big bulk come charging out of the deeper darkness of the buildings lining one side of the ramp. A twelve-hundred pound bull would have nothing on him, the way he came galloping. His reflexes were quick too. Though I side-stepped his crouching lunge, his shoulder took me in the middle, jackknifing me and sending me back toward the low wall across the ramp. My legs struck it and my back went up on it and for a moment I thought Paco wouldn't even have to work up a sweat. But I teetered there, not going over to decorate the lower level of the ramp with the remains of Chester Drum, and then Paco's momentum brought him to me. I planted both feet against his chest and shoved. I'd been right: he was big and he was fast, and as easy to knock over as a cross-country van.

Still, I checked him, and he even moved back a foot, giving me time to climb off the wall. He swung wildly. I went in under that, not having to crouch though I'm six-one, and planted a good one in his middle. It was supposed to bend him, setting him up for a shot at his long slab of a jaw. Only it didn't. Again it stopped him, that was all. He took a breath and swung again and missed again. He swung hard enough to put his fist through a bull-ring's barera. If he landed once, that was all it would take. He knew it and I knew it, and the unpleasant notion that my fists wouldn't be able to stop him occurred to me.

He swung a third time, missing a third time. I went under it again, in there trying again, and while I was planting the same right in his gut, with the same disappointing effect, though I'm nobody's cream-puff, he brought his hand toward me again, backhanded after the follow-through, and this time he hit. I sailed back and landed on my duff against the low wall. He loomed there, as big as two picadors sitting one on the other's shoulders and both on horseback. He kicked. I moved my head and he didn't quite kick the wall down. But it shook, brother; it shook.

That was when I scrambled to my feet and said the hell with it and drew the gun. It was a small, neat Beretta, and though it could drill a small neat hole in Paco's head, that still wasn't what I wanted. I held it by the barrel and when he uncorked one of his wild swings, each one closer than the last because I was slowing down, I let him have the butt against his mouth.

He cried out, like a bull bellowing from an inept sword thrust, and sprayed blood at me. I smashed the Beretta against the side of his jaw. He sagged to his knees and wrapped his arms around my middle, almost bringing me down on top of him. I brought the Beretta down on top of his skull. He fell the rest of the way reluctantly, but he fell.

Though he wasn't out, he was all finished killing me for the night.

I heard running footfalls. His bellow of pain had summoned the Guardia. "Next time," he sobbed, trying to get up but unable to manage it, "I use my pick."

"Next time," I told him, "I'll try bullets."

Maruja crouched over him, gently touching his face. She looked up at me, letting loose a string of curses in Spanish that would have made an old monosabio, who had heard most but not all of them, blush from the knees up.

I heard the Guardia trotting down from the direction of the Calle San Miguel. He blew his whistle as I ran the other way, back toward the beach. Then through the rushes and across the sand and down past the cliffs and finally up to the highway that ran back of Carihuela so I could return to the Hartshorn villa, wondering all the while why I didn't stay home and pick up a retainer on an easy case, like busting up the Syndicate single-handed.

chapter fifteen

I found Andrea Hartshorn where I knew I'd find her in the morning, out on the terrace watching her own private sunrise. I'd slept in my room of the guest wing of La Atalaya, the Beretta under my pillow, half expecting the Guardia to come there looking for me. But nobody ever found Poe's purloined letter, did they? I'd told myself they did, eventually, and I'd almost decided to grab my shuteye out in the open somewhere, where I could run for it if I had to, but the next thing I knew the dawn was on its way and no hard, heavy Guardia hand had stirred me ungently out of sleep. So I shaved, showered, got into some clean clothes and went to find Andrea.

After the sun burst up over the horizon and after she greeted it with solemn, ritual silence, she said, "I didn't know you came back last night. The maids described a man who was in the kitchen with Tenley. It had to be you, Chet." She smiled. "They think you're handsome, even with a sprouting barba and with rumpled, dirty ropas as they put it. Where did you and Tenley go?"

"Isn't she here?"

"No. She took the MG last night. Or early this morning, rather. I assumed you went with her."

"Not me."

Andrea scowled. "That's funny. I—I'm worried about her, Chet. She's usually self-sufficient and so damn capable and confident you think nothing can touch her. But lately she—would you know if she had a lovers' tiff with Ruy Fuentes? Do you think she's there now, in Fuengirola?"

"He had an accident in the bull ring. She may have gone there to be with him, yes."

That interpretation of the situation seemed to make Andrea feel better. She nodded and said, "Tenley's nothing if not loyal." But self-pity dragged down the corners of her mouth. "Out of loyalty she came back here to Robbie and me, back from Switzerland, and we didn't deserve it. Lord knows we haven't been the world's best parents to her. She could have gone back home to her Grandfather and .... don't mind me. It's one of those blue mornings. I need a drink. I always need a drink."

"I need transportation," I said.

She looked her age in the dark, long shadows of early morning. Her eyes were pouched and her mouth bitter. She tugged at my sleeve. Her fingers were trembling. A couple of ounces of Fundador neat, I thought, feeling sorry for her, would cure that.

"Please don't go yet," she said. "Please have a drink with me. I'm not like Tenley. I'm not self-sufficient. I hate to be alone." She had no image of herself at all. She could be as solitary as a cat or as communal as a bee, depending on whether liquor and her need for it lifted her or dropped her. "This is going to be one of those bad mornings," she said. "Do you think you'll find Robbie? Tell me about it over a drink?"

"I'd better go," I said.

She sighed. "You can have Robbie's car. It's the Mercedes Benz 220S parked in the carport downstairs. I'll get you the keys."

It took her ten minutes to get them. When she returned, her eyes were bright and she smiled at me. I could smell the Fundador. "One set of car keys for one enterprising private eye," she said, giving them to me. "You'd make a good remittance man, Chet. You always seem to have something to do with your time. That's the trouble with us, with all of us here. Sometimes I feel like screaming, listening to the seconds drag by."

Liquored up, she wanted to talk even more than when she'd needed a drink. "I once dreamed an hour fell on me. It was on the biggest clock in the world and it just fell off and pinned me. I couldn't move it. I kicked and clawed at it, and I knew if I didn't get it off I'd be forever under that one hour. Did you know that people sometimes die in their sleep because they have dreams too horrible for their subconscious minds to stand?" She said stonily, "You're not listening. You have only contempt for me, don't you? I guess nobody really likes anybody else. We all just make believe, and it's easier that way." She sobbed. "I feel so naked sometimes. I know I'm no good, and I know everybody can see it. Except with Robbie. We were always so good together. We were the only people in the world who understood each other. There was no time for anything else, not even Tenley." She grabbed my sleeve again. "Please don't go yet."

I felt embarrassed for her, standing there in the early morning with one of the world's beautiful views as a backdrop, whitewashed walls and tile roofs and fat palms

and the blue sea and the gulf curving off toward Malaga
nestling at the foothills of the high Sierra Nevadas
crowned with snow, and she in a whisky-jaded world of
confusion and self-pity and that special alcoholic bore-
dom that, if you're neither careful nor lucky nor rich,
can lead to a padded cell.

"I've got to get going," I said.

She called after me, "You want to know something? I
hate this goddamn sunrise. Every morning, and I hate it.
Isn't that a laugh? I actually detest it."

Her bitter dissatisfaction followed me down the long
flight of stairs like a terrier nipping at my heels.

Eyes wide open, I drove right into it.

The 220S was gun-metal gray and handled beautifully.
For no reason at all, I opened her up on the corniche
drive to Fuengirola. She whispered along, a dream of a
car, hitting eighty on the short straightaways between
hairpin bends, taking the curves as if on tracks, rumbling-
ly absorbing the shock of potholes as if they weren't
there.

I left the highway and drove up into the hills, telling
myself Tenley first, because if she didn't watch out she
could be one of the lost ones like her mother. Maybe I
couldn't help that but I could try, and maybe what Ruy
Fuentes did or didn't do wouldn't matter either, but it
was all inside Tenley—as it is all inside all of us—waiting
to give her joy or to make her suffer. And after Tenley,
the mountain city of Ronda, where Spain's fighting bulls
are bred and where smugglers—not to mention highjackers—transship their cargoes, because that was where
Fernando was heading for a showdown with Pez Espada,
and when the fireworks go off truth rears its sometimes
ugly head, so maybe I'd learn what had happened to
Robbie Hartshorn.

His 220S came to a purring stop outside the caves of
Fuentes. As I got out I wondered why he hadn't driven
there himself. He'd taken the bus, Andrea had told me.
Because he hadn't expected to return? It didn't make
sense. Because he'd been too drunk to drive? But why
wouldn't he have waited, unless it was urgent?

I went into the smaller cave first. It had a door, the
door wasn't locked and the furniture looked as if it be-

longed in a big villa on a high hill. "Hello?" I called. "Anybody home?" The light approach, the casual entrance, but I remembered Paco and my hand was on the butt of the Beretta. No answer. There were four rooms, one of them a dining room. Dishes on the table, not cleared yet. Service for two, and a pot of cold paella that still smelled good. In the sink, service for three, and that meal had been paella too and it had been eaten. The dishes there were scraped but not washed. Figure it out, Drum. Three: that would be Maruja and the Fuentes brothers, and they ate, and then Maruja and Paco went off, together, to La Atalaya for Fernando and then with him to Carihuela. Which left Ruy. Then paella for two on the table. Meaning Tenley had arrived? I decided she had, only they hadn't eaten. Not that they didn't want to. Something had snatched them away from the table in a hurry. What? I didn't know what.

I poked around the rest of the place. It was just a home, and a well-furnished one, in a cave. Unusual, but I wasn't looking for that kind of unusual. There were standing closets in the two bedrooms, Maruja's clothes in one and the Fuentes brothers' in the other. Nothing had been packed. They'd left in a hurry, all right.

Outside again. The sunlight by then was dazzling. I shaded my eyes and headed for the bigger cave, first stopping at the 220S, opening the trunk and taking a screwdriver from the tool-kit. With it I ought to be able to pry loose the staples holding the overhead door in place. But when I reached it, I found that wasn't necessary. The lock was on the floor of the cave, opened. I picked it up, hooked it through the staple in the door and yanked up hard.

The heavy door slid gratingly toward the roof of the cave.

Light flared on in front of my eyes, blinding me. I groped for the Beretta, found it and drew it.

"Drop the gun, Señor Drum," a wistful voice said in Spanish. "We can see you and you can't see us. There are three rifles trained on you, held by men who know how to shoot and who will shoot if they have to. Drop it!"

The gun clattered to the floor. There was nothing else I could do. I still couldn't see them, and with those lights shining on me they'd be able to see the nick where I'd cut my chin shaving.

The wistful voice, of course, belonged to Sergeant Martinez.

chapter sixteen

The light came from the high beams of a Guardia Seat in the cave. Someone cut them, and while I blinked Sergeant Martinez stepped out past the fender of the car, giving me his Don Quixote smile but still managing to look unhappy.

"You could have saved yourself the trouble," I said. "Why didn't you pick me up at La Atalaya?"

"It is no longer necessary," he said, wistfully and sadly. "There never was a denunciation—now. You are a free man—now."

I saw the rifles watching me—two on one side of the Seat and one on the other. "Then if I'm a free man, will you have those things pointed some other way?"

He barked an order. The rifles were lowered.

"I thought of your advice," he said. He shrugged. "I followed it. What else could I do?"

"What advice would that be?"

"Rafael Jímenez. The cousin of Doña Maruja, who lives in Carihuela. Two agents of the Guardia went there. The fisherman Jímenez tried to stop them, but they examined his boat. It has a high-powered American engine. A Chrysler of three-hundred horses. My agents were not—gentle with him. He broke quickly. The Fuentes brothers, they used his boat. To meet the smugglers running contraband along the coast from Gibraltar. To highjack their cargoes." He said with bitter accusation, "Not to help the little people, the poor ones who invest their pesetas, but to make them lose their money. I am a disillusioned man, Señor Drum. Sometimes the truth—"

"Who were you waiting here for?"

"Quién sabe? Americans and my own people, they are all in it. Rafael Jímenez broke down, as I have said, and cried in his fear and grief to the Virgin—and talked. The brothers, they run the boat. The brothers, they drive the contraband through the mountains to Ronda." He laughed bitterly. "With agents of the Guardia passing them through all along the route, as everyone knew they were smugglers and all the world on this coast loves a smuggler. Smugglers! They were highjackers."

"Who else is in it?" I said.

"The blind artist, Fernando. He handles gems for them. An American named Short in Torremolinos, who owns a souvenir shop. He sells the figurines where the jewels are hidden. He has been picked up, along with a list of his buyers. The dead man, Huntington. He was part of it too. As you said, he had been murdered. Why, I do not know. Jímenez did not know him, but the name meant much. Pez Espada in Algeciras and Huntington here, he said. Between them they ran the ring. Apparently Huntington wanted too much for himself, and Pez Espada objected. Huntington's original investment was the boat. He refitted it and supplied the engine, though Jímenez never saw him. But Huntington had lived in Spain since the war, and he had many contacts. His job was to arrange for the disposal of the contraband all over my country."

"What happened to the Fuentes brothers? And Maruja."

Martinez shook his head sadly, wistfully. "Late last night I sent two agents. They had the misfortune to meet Paco at the bottom of the hill. They shined a flashlight on his face and he looked bloody and injured, and that deceived them. Both are now in the hospital at Malaga. The Fuentes brothers, the gypsy and their truck—all are gone."

And Tenley, I thought. Tenley, too.

"Pez Espada," Martinez went on, "he left Algeciras before the Guardia there could arrest him. I had hoped he might come here. I had hoped Fernando Robles might." He grinned at me, and this time the grin was only wistful and not at all sad. "I had hoped to snare something besides an ally in my little trap, amigo."

"Then try setting it in Ronda. Fernando's on his way there—to see Pez Espada."

The wistfulness finally left his smile. He looked like a hungry wolf ready to pounce on its prey, his lips and jaw in a wide grin but his eyes flinty. "They have cost me my career," he said. "Because naturally my complicity will be revealed—how I took money to permit the smugglers to

operate along the coast. But if they were only smugglers
. . . . if at least my conscience before God and my people
had been clear . . . . but now it is of no importance. Of no
importance."

"You going to Ronda?"

He grew wistful again. "My last official act. I should call
the Guardia station there, but I won't do it. There is
nothing they can do that I cannot, and it is only a two-
hour drive through the mountains. I will get them, señor.
And for a few moments, before better policemen than I
take them in, I will make them wish they had not deceived me. This I vow."

"You're not going alone," I said.

He misunderstood. "Naturally not. I have these two
agents, and when we reach Ronda I can get more."

"I'm driving up there in the Mercedes."

He shrugged. "As I said, you are a free man. The road
to Ronda is open. But if Pez Espada or the Fuentes brothers become desperate, they may be shooting."

So far as I knew, Tenley was up there with Ruy Fuentes. Martinez was right: Pez Espada wouldn't be about to
throw in the towel at the first sign of a green Guardia uniform or a winged patent-leather hat, not with one murder rap and maybe two hanging over his head. Neither
would the Fuentes brothers. As for Martinez, he'd face
the ruin of his own life easier if he could clobber the men
who'd brought it about. Either way, and especially both
ways, Tenley might be caught in the cross fire.

"There may be shooting," Martinez said again.

"Why do you think I'm driving up there?" I said.

chapter seventeen

In Robbie Hartshorn's powerful 220S I followed the
Guardia Seat, impatient at its lack of speed, impatient
at the slow way it accelerated off curves, impatient at
the way it struggled up the steep mountain road once
we left the coast to head north a few miles out of Marbella.

The narrow, unpaved road climbed and twisted,
corkscrewing up into the hills. At first there were only

the cork forests and wind-stunted pines, but suddenly pulling out of a switchback I could see the whole sweep of the Costa Del Sol and the turquoise Mediterranean and, with a mist at its base, Gibraltar hanging like a mirage out toward the horizon. Then, higher, that view too was gone, and the sheer rock walls of canyons loomed on all sides. We passed no cars coming down, and except for an occasional shack where the patroling Guardia could rest, there was nothing to indicate that men ever passed this way. There are mountains far higher than those guarding Ronda; there may be wilder country. But in any part of the world that calls itself civilized there is no serpentine stretch of road like that leading to a city perched on a cliff like an eagle's aerie.

After almost two hours of that, the road straightened out. It began to drop gradually into a cool and wind-swept mountain valley, and after the sheer canyons the vistas there seemed vast. Ahead of me, the Seat veered left around an outcropping of rock. When I followed it around the curve, I saw Ronda. Far in the distance on its circular cliff it looked like a fairy city on a giant toadstool. Its buildings were white and dun-colored. They seemed to have been carved from the rock of the cliff. And just when you thought the whole setup was too mathematically perfect to be real—the round city on its round cliff exactly in the center of its round valley called the Serena—you saw the chasm. It was the deep cleft of a river's gorge, and it bisected the city. The windows of buildings on either side of the gorge stared across at each other. An old stone bridge spanned its awesome depths. You told yourself, hey, that damn thing must be eight hundred feet deep, and then the road was paved again and began to climb up from the floor of the valley of the Serena to where Ronda was waiting.

Sergeant Martinez wasn't the only Guardia living off his winged patent-leather hat, and once he decided—sensibly—to get reinforcements, we learned that.

We parked both cars in a plaza near a small white church. The bells in their tower bonged ten times, the sun was strong but the air cool. Two cowled nuns left the church and crossed our path. Sergeant Martinez doffed his hat. A pair of early-rising tourists, each armed with the inevitable camera, stopped to take our picture: Martinez and his two Guardia agents in their green uniforms and patent-leather hats and the pair of nuns, with the scrubbed white church as a background.

"Hey, buddy," one of them asked me, "will you like step off to one side? You spoil the picture."

I like stepped off to one side, while Martinez and his sidekicks had their pictures taken. Then we crossed the plaza and climbed some steps and went in under the sign that said *Toda por la Patria*.

Because Ronda was the center not only of bull-breeding, horse-breeding and mule-breeding, but of the Spanish smugglers' world as well, it was a large Guardia station in the biggest building on the square. Green uniforms came and went, patent-leather hats were clapped on and taken off, boots glistened and stomped on tile floors. A surly-looking little man with a black-and-blue jaw and a torn shirt and puffed lips was slouching before the duty-desk. The sergeant behind it paid him no attention at all. Then another sergeant came down the stairs to the left of the desk, took one look at the little man, sauntered casually over to him and, swinging from the shoulder, hit him open-palmed as hard as he could in the left ear. The little man fell down and stood up, and the sergeant hit him again and he fell down again. Then the sergeant called him three or four choice Spanish words and stamped his heel on the fallen man's groin. The little man screamed and rolled into a ball, clutching his private parts.

"I know that one," Martinez told me as the sergeant sauntered just as casually out. "He is a pickpocket. He used to work the férias and bullfights along the coast until we chased him. That was after his last time in prison, and apparently he is back to his old tricks, this time in Ronda. We do not like pickpockets. They discourage the tourists."

The little pickpocket stood up, crouching in pain. Aside from that, he waited there as if nothing had happened to him.

As we went up the stairs, Martinez told me, "I have a friend here. Lieutenant Velasquez, a good man. He will believe this of the highjacking when I tell him. He will give us what help we need. Out of Ronda there are but three roads. If we block all three, and if we send a task force to Pez Espada's town house on the river gorge—"

"Doesn't he have a ranch for bull-breeding? Wouldn't that be in Serena, outside the city?"

Martinez smiled calmly. "He sold his ranch, years ago. To an American who—" Suddenly Martinez's eyes narrowed and he stood still on the stairs. "The American, he was this man Huntington. They could be using the ranch."

"They'd almost have to use it," I said. "They'd need a place to store the contraband they drive up here from Fuengirola. If they stored it inside the city, they'd have to pass the Guardia check-points going in and out."

"Something that is done, in Ronda, every day." Martinez sighed. "I know what it is like to take money from smugglers."

"But wouldn't it be easier outside?"

"Yes," Martinez admitted. "It would be easier. I will ask Velasquez what he thinks."

But when he reached the top of the stairs and the floor of offices there, he didn't ask Velasquez that or anything. Velasquez, they told him, had been transferred to Valladolid. We saw a man named Diaz de la Frontera instead. He was a young, shiny-faced man in a lieutenant's uniform. He had large front teeth, like a rabbit's. He used them to munch on his lower lip while he listened gravely to our story, his small, wide-spaced eyes searching my face and Martinez's as if he expected to find more truth there than in the words we spoke.

When we finished, he said in a high voice, "But this man Manzanarez, that you call Pez Espada, is well-known in Ronda; one of our leading citizens, though the last few years he has lived much on the coast in Algeciras. He is known and respected in Ronda, as was his father before him. Their family used to breed the finest fighting bulls in all Spain."

"But now they don't?" I asked.

He shook his head mournfully. "No señor. Five-year-olds it used to be. But now the bulls are removed from the ranches to the bull rings at four and even three years, and the younger Manzanarez, that you call Pez

Espada, decided this was not a running of the bulls, it was butchery. He sold his ranch to an American—"

"Who breeds what?"

"Why, nothing, señor," said Diaz de la Frontera. "Rarely is he seen on the ranch. I heard he was killed in an automobile accident on the coast. Qué lástima! Such a pity!"

"Pez Espada didn't think so. Neither did the Fuentes brothers. Pez Espada had him killed, and the Fuentes brothers did the killing."

Diaz de la Frontera's shiny face turned a faint shade of pink. "That is what you say, señor, but we here in Ronda have known Señor Manzanarez too long to believe—"

"What was he doing in Algeciras, lieutenant?"

Diaz de la Frontera smiled a shiny, baby-faced smile. "That is his business. If as you say he was breaking the law, that is the business of the Guardia in Algeciras. Not ours here in Ronda."

"Under the cover of agenting the kind of smuggling you don't frown on, he was setting up smugglers' cargo to be highjacked," I said.

"You have made that accusation already," he said. "You haven't proved it to my satisfaction."

"But to mine, lieutenant," Sergeant Martinez said. He was staring out the window at the white church with his hands clenched stiffly at his sides.

"I say we cannot bother Señor Manzanarez with such accusations."

Martinez turned slowly. "I say we must."

The younger man said, a little crisply, "May I remind you, sergeant, that I am a commissioned officer in the service you dishonor with your disrespect for my uniform?"

"And may I remind you, lieutenant," Martinez shot right back, looking like Don Quixote for the first time since we'd entered the office, "that I wore this uniform while you were still running around with a bare bottom —sir?"

"I say we cannot bother—"

"I say we must. Sir."

"Listen, lieutenant," I pointed out. "We're here because we think we can prove it. I can and will testify that Huntington was murdered in Fuengirola. I can and will testify that the American MacPherson, also murdered, was carrying six brands of cigarettes, three hundred cartons each. Unless I miss my guess, you'll find them on Pez Espada's ranch."

"Huntington's ranch, señor. Pez Espada sold it."

"Good for him. We also have the confession of an American named Short, who disposed of the smuggled gems. We also have the confession of Rafael Jímenez, whose fishing boat, powered by a motor Huntington supplied, did the highjacking. But go ahead, lieutenant. Live off your patent-leather hat another day or two. Use your head. They'll give you a medal for cleaning this up. You'll find another smuggler to feed you dinero."

"Is that an accusation?" he demanded in a high, angry voice. "Who are you? By what authority do you come in here . . . how dare you come in here and accuse me of complicity . . . if Sergeant Martinez wishes to disgrace his uniform . . . but you, a foreigner with no authority. . . ." The more he spoke, the madder he got. His small eyes narrowed until they almost shut. His shiny face, the plump cheeks looking like polished apples, was shinier with sweat. His speech was almost incoherent.

Sergeant Martinez said wistfully, "We can go ourselves to the ranch. It is true, as the lieutenant may perhaps wish, that we may not return alive. But if we do, and if we find what is to be found there, and if I make a deposition that the lieutenant not only failed to help a fellow Guardia agent but in fact hampered him—"

"I can order your men to remain behind," Diaz de la Frontera threatened. The two Guardia agents were waiting downstairs.

"Yes, sir. You can. I can put that in my deposition as well."

"I can have you charged with insubordination," fumed Diaz de la Frontera.

"Naturally, sir. My deposition—"

"That is enough of you and your deposition."

Diaz de la Frontera glared. Martinez smiled wistfully. Franco beamed down paternally at them from the wall.

"I will go with you," Diaz de la Frontera said at last.

"With a car full of Guardia agents," Martinez said.

"Armed to the teeth," I said, "so Pez Espada gets the

idea he'd better not fight. There's a young girl with them, lieutenant."

He rubbed his hands together. He mopped his sweating face. "A car . . . half a dozen agents . . . riot guns. All that will take time."

"Ten minutes," said Martinez.

"An hour at least!"

"Ten minutes," said Martinez implacably. "Sir."

"Ten minutes," sighed Diaz de la Frontera.

He told us to go downstairs and wait. I wasn't wild about that, but it was his office. Even in just ten minutes there was plenty he could do.

chapter eighteen

The surly little man still stood in his half crouch before the duty-desk. When the day aged five minutes, a pair of Guardia with riot guns sauntered in from a back room and began to pass the time of day with Martinez's two agents. Another five minutes, and another pair of Guardia with riot guns. They all lounged and slouched around, a couple of them smoking and one of them needing a shave. They didn't look like any Buckingham Palace guards.

Sergeant Martinez gave Diaz de la Frontera fifteen minutes. When he hadn't come downstairs by then, Martinez scowled at me and started climbing up to fetch him.

He got halfway and stopped. One of the fattest men I have ever seen stomped ponderously down the stairs. He filled them from wall to bannister. The green uniform stretched across his belly looked as big as a circus tent. He had three chins, each lower one wider than the one above it and each with its own dewlaps. He was smoking one of those twisted black cigars Spaniards like. Assorted silver braid and medals festooned his uniform.

Martinez stood still, and the fat man kept coming downstairs. His belly bumped Martinez from chin to waist, and Martinez backed downstairs.

"You!" boomed the fat man in a voice like Krakatau blowing its volcanic lid. "You, sergeant from Fuengirola!" he roared, making Fuengirola sound like the butt end of the universe. "You have no jurisdiction here. No authority here."

"Yes, my colonel," Martinez said in a subdued voice.

"I am not your colonel," shouted the colonel, waving an enormous dimpled fist before his face. "Such a one as you would never serve in my command. To attempt to give orders to one of my commissioned officers," spluttered the fat man in a mounting rage, "that is insubordination. I can have your stripes for it, sergeant. I will."

"But my colonel—"

The colonel's voice rushed over his words like a waterfall rushing over its brink. "You shut up! No words! No explanations! I am holding you for disciplinary action. Holding you! Before I'm finished, you'll be patroling on a bicycle on the road past Estepona."

"If, my colonel, you will permit me to explain—"

"Explain that," said the fat man, and hit him in the face with a dimpled fist. Sergeant Martinez didn't go down, but his knees buckled. The surly pickpocket's puffed lips moved above his black and blue jaw, and a noise like a sighing hiccup issued from his mouth. I realized he was laughing. The fat colonel shouted some more. Martinez stood very straight and took it. Then the fat colonel squawked an order, and the four Guardia took their riot guns back where they'd got them and returned empty-handed. The fat colonel chewed them out for their slovenliness, for the sprouting beard one of them had, for their smoking on duty, for their compliance with orders that had not come from him. They grew pale listening, lined up like four little Indians in a row as he paced back and forth in front of them, fat hands clasped behind him above his enormous bottom, fat head turning on fat neck to spit his words at one or another of them.

Then back to Martinez, "We're holding you. We're contacting Fuengirola. Who is your superior there?"

"It is only a substation, my colonel. I am in charge."

"*You* are in charge?"

"Yes, my colonel. I—"

"You *were* in charge. I'll contact Malaga. Madrid, if I must. My officers are not to be intimidated by. . . ."

There was more of it, a great deal more, but never once was Pez Espada mentioned, or the Fuentes brothers, or blind Fernando, or any of the things that had brought

Martinez up the mountain road to Ronda. He never got more than a dozen words in edgewise, and those only ineffectually and with effort. The fat man completely dominated him. Finally two of the Guardia marched him away, past the duty-desk and through a doorway. He looked back over his shoulder at me, wistful, apologetic.

I glanced at the fat colonel. He was breathing hard, his dewlaps quivering. I didn't know what I could do alone, but one of me was better than none of nobody. Slowly, casually, I started for the street door.

"You, Englishman! Wait where you are!" bawled the fat man.

I corrected him as to my nationality. That usually placates a Spaniard, especially in uniform, especially in the south. They hate the English for Gibraltar, which they think ought to be a Spanish rock guarding a Spanish sea. They like Americans.

But nothing was going to placate the fat colonel. Maybe he really was worked up over the treatment Diaz de la Frontera had received; maybe he had a fat colonel-sized investment to protect. I never learned which. He bawled me out in a mixture of Spanish and English, his face getting redder and redder, his voice louder and louder. I was a meddler. I was a fool. I was a stranger in Spain with no business but to see the sights and buy a ticket in the shade at a bullfight. Did I not know this? Surely all the world knew it. What I waited for, almost with a sense of detached interest, was for him to thrust his fat hand out and ask to see my passport. I didn't have my passport. The Guardia in Fuengirola still had it. In Spain, especially if you are in trouble, you do not wander around without identification.

He never asked for it. He didn't have me searched either. The casual touch of a hand would have uncovered the Beretta in my belt. All he wanted to do was put me on ice. Merely to sock me for having helped give Diaz de la Frontera a hard time? To give Pez Espada the chance to do whatever he had come to Ronda to do, now that Rafael Jímenez and the American named Short were talking? The latter seemed more likely. Leaving truckloads of contraband behind, even if half the Guardia was on the take, seemed no way for Pez Espada to establish his innocence.

Compared with the one in Fuengirola, the Ronda lock-up was a de luxe suite in a luxury hotel. The cell they locked me in had running cold water, a dirty and foul-smelling blanket on the bedspring and a rusty, battered bucket for sanitary purposes. It also had a view out over the plaza to the white church. I stood at the barred window and watched half a dozen urchins admiring Robbie Hartshorn's Mercedez Benz. The same two American tourists posed the kids there and snapped their pictures of the contrast: five thousand bucks worth of car and kids who didn't have a peseta among them.

Noon came. The door opened, and I was given a tin plate of cold, greasy beans that had been cooked in rancid olive oil. I dozed off for a while. When I awoke, the shadows had lengthened in the plaza. I looked at my watch. It was two o'clock. Siesta, and the plaza deserted. I heard laughter in another part of the building. The rest of the cells in the lockup block were empty. I stared at the walls and the bars. I scratched my leg and kept scratching it and realized there were lice in the blanket. I threw it off the bed and sat on the bare bedspring, still scratching.

You should have argued with the fat man, I told myself. Told him you were working for the governor of Maryland, which you were, or some damn thing like that. Put the fear of Uncle in him. Lockup thoughts, while the afternoon grew hot and hung like a five-hundred-watt bulb over my head. Then, as it became cooler, I knew arguing would have been a mistake. Let him dish it out. Take it. I couldn't have done anything else. If I'd got all hot and bothered, to match his being all hot and bothered, he might have decided to have a look at my passport. But my passport was in Fuengirola. Then they'd have really thrown the key away.

Five o'clock. Siesta over and the crowds thronging the plaza. The same kids, or a fresh batch of them, poked around the Mercedes. Nobody took their picture.

At sundown they came for me, two Guardia I hadn't seen before. They opened the cell door, and one of them walked with me and one behind me as we went along a hall and down the stairs. Finally, the pickpocket was gone. They hadn't taken him to the lockup, or Sergeant Martinez either for that matter. I wondered what had happened to them. I didn't see the fat colonel. I didn't see Diaz de la Frontera. I was escorted to the street door and through it.

"You are free to go," one of the Guardia said in English. "The colonel says to tell you if you do not leave Ronda before dark," he added, the words heavily accented and hard to understand, "you are being in bad trouble."

"It's almost dark now."

"Before dark, hombre."

So I went obediently over to the Mercedes. That impressed the Guardia. They hadn't known it was my car. Come to think of it, it wasn't. An afternoon in their lockup, and already I had an inferiority complex.

I drove fast for three blocks, hit a labyrinth of crooked streets, got lost, found a wide plaza in front of the bull ring, that was the oldest one in Spain, parked and asked the uniformed guarda-coche who was dusting off the windshield of a Citroën if he knew the way to the Manzanarez ranch. He knew, and he told me.

It was probably too late, or the fat colonel would have kept me on ice overnight.

The only trouble was, I had nowhere else to go.

chapter nineteen

At dusk the great black vultures of the Serena rise on the thermal up-drafts of the valley and soar effortlessly, wings unmoving, to the heights of Ronda on its cliff. Bats emerge too, fluttering like wet black paper from tree to tree. By then the last tourists, those who aren't staying overnight at the Hotel Victoria, have long-since started back down the road to the coast. To drive the roads into and out of Ronda at night, when darkness cloaks the unbanked curves, the potholes and the giddy abrupt hills, is to take your life in your hands.

I left the city on the road that dropped southward to the coast at Marbella. Six kilometers through the Serena, the guarda-coche had told me. Half a kilometer before the road begins to climb up through the mountains, preparing to swoop down from this tierra on the very heights of the world to the coast, you will see a narrow track on the right. That is the way to the ranch where the Manzanarez family used to breed the best fighting bulls in all Spain.

With the last faint daylight still in the sky, I found the turn-off. It was unpaved and narrow. Centuries of melting snow rushing down from the heights had eroded its surface, scarring it with gullies, pitting it, making it treacherous with fallen rocks. The Mercedes bucked, rumbled, skidded and slid. I had to hold the wheel tight with both hands, peering intently at the headlight beams to pick out and avoid the worst of the ruts and rocks.

Five minutes like that, and then I saw headlights ahead of me. They were coming fast, far too fast for that road at night. If I saw them, they had to see me. I slowed down. They didn't. I leaned on the horn. They kept coming. There wouldn't be room for both of us.

To left and right the road-shoulder fell away steeply for a few yards before leveling off among boulders and big cacti. I leaned on the horn again. Suddenly I realized we were in a drag race. They weren't going to stop. They wanted the right of way hard enough to fight for it.

I cut may speed to twenty, then to fifteen, then ten with the Mercedes in second gear. Between their headlights I could see, with the Mercedes' lights on it, the figure of a smiling, scantily-clad girl skating—the emblem of a Peggaso truck. Smiling, with a spotlight on either side of her, she skated slantwise at me. With how many tons of truck behind her?

When she was almost in my lap I braked hard and swung the wheel to the left. Something struck the rear fender of the Mercedes glancingly and it wobbled on the shoulder of the road like a drunk in a barrel at an amusement park. Then it picked up speed going down the incline, and then I was breaking and dodging boulders. A final slewing skid and I came to a stop, gently nudging a boulder half the size of the car. I got out. I saw the taillights of the truck. It might be heading for Ronda. It might be heading for the coast. Pez Espada behind the wheel? Or fat Estebán and the tough little Spaniard, Diego? The Fuentes brothers? Whoever they were, they

were in a hurry. A little detail like a moving car block-
ing the road wasn't going to stop them.

I climbed into the Mercedes, sawing it back and forth
among the rocks, tires squealing, dust flying, engine
groaning, until I was facing the road. All in a sweat,
all in a lather, but when I mounted the shoulder I realized by then they'd have hit what passed for the highway
that ran down from Ronda to the coast. Had they turned
south into the mountains or north across the Serena?
I sat there with my night thoughts: next time win
your drag race, buddy. Next time, if they've got four
tons of Peggaso behind them, use a Sherman tank.

Then, to my left, I saw a glow in the night sky. That
was where the ranch was, and the glow could only be
a fire. I turned left and drove fast. The glow flickered
and pulsed brighter.

It was a long, low building crumbling slowly and pic-
turesquely to ruin, the stucco walls cracked and scabby
in the firelight, the front door hanging open on one hinge,
a pile of bricks among the cacti in the front yard that
might once have been a chimney struck by lightning,
the glass in the windows broken and reflecting flames
inside. There was a large outbuilding to the left, its
barn doors yawning wide, and beyond that a corral, the
fence-posts still standing but most of the rails down. If
Manzanarez hadn't bred bulls for a number of years,
and apparently he hadn't, the hard Serena winters had
done their work. And the fire, in a night, would finish it.

Smoke roiled from the door, tongues of flame licked
hungrily out the windows. A beam gave way inside and
a crack appeared under a window to the left of the
door. Part of the tile roof fell in.

A man's voice bellowed with fear—that terrible, final
fear of death by bright fire.

The sound of his voice drew me toward the door.
The heat hit me like a wall, and then I was inside.

The fire had started in the left wing of the ranch-
house and though smoke had reached the main hallway,
flames hadn't. I stood there, choking in the smoke, my
eyes watering, waiting for his voice again.

"Where are you?" I shouted in Spanish.

This time he only groaned and coughed. I heard a scraping sound, wood moving heavily over tile, to my left. There was an archway there, smoke billowing from it, flames darting.

Then I saw him. He was big, and he was roped hand and foot to a chair, and he'd managed to overturn it and was dragging himself, chair and all, an inch at a time across the tile floor. He'd reached the threshold under the archway. I went to him through the smoke and got hold of the chair and dragged it across the tile to the front door and outside. I felt a muscle knot low in my back. He weighed a ton.

He was Paco Fuentes. A spark smouldered in his hair. The breeze outside fanned it and suddenly his hair began to burn brightly. He screamed. I beat the flames out with my hands. I could smell his burned hair. He hadn't been hurt, though. The scream was of fear.

He began to groan. He couldn't see me. His eyes were puffy from the smoke.

"Anybody else in there?" I said.

He didn't answer.

"Who else is in there?" I shouted.

When he still didn't answer, I hit him. He was over on his side, still roped to the chair. A sliver of bloodshot eye stared up at me.

"Ruy," he said. "Ruy is inside."

I went back for him. I was going on reflexes then. A man is in a burning house, roped, helpless. You're the only one who can help. You look at the smoke and the fire, and the sweat of fear stings your eyes. But you go.

Bright flames danced at the archway. I ducked through and felt nothing special, just the heat all around me, just the smoke searching for my lungs. One try, I thought, as long as you hold your breath. The house was going. Something cracked, something else thudded and roof tiles crashed at my feet.

"Ruy!" I shouted.

I heard him then, a whimper. It led me through the smoke, and I could see him. He hadn't been able to overturn his chair that he was roped to, as his brother had done. He sat there, eyes swollen shut, head bowed in the smoke. No flame had touched him yet, and at first that didn't make sense. If whoever was driving the Peg-gaso had set the fire, and if part of its purpose was to incinerate the Fuentes brothers, why not set it where it would get them in a hurry? Then, dragging Ruy's chair out, I knew. Because it might have got to the ropes that bound them first. This way, smoke-poisoning first and then if the ropes burned through it wouldn't matter.

I reached the archway and backed through it, drag-ging him. Then out of the house and far enough away to be safe. Was Paco far enough? I looked, and saw that he was. Ruy shouted hoarsely. I lurched over to him. His pants were starting to burn. I rolled him while he yelled, and kept rolling him till the fire was out. Then I sat for a long time and drew my knees up and thrust my head between them and breathed and listened to the thud of my heart and with mild tangential interest watched the flutter of my fingers. Behind us, bright in the night, flames wreathed and then enveloped the long, low building.

"Pez Espada," Paco said hoarsely while I unfastened the ropes that bound him. "His villa in Ronda. On the cliff, near the bridge of stone. You say you have come for the pretty Americana with afición. She is there. I will show you the way. Take me there."

Ruy, who was already free, glared down at him. "Don't be a fool," he said. "We can't return there now," he added in Spanish. "Not with the American."

Paco glanced at his right hand. The skin was puck-ered and blistered. "This was an execution, my brother," he said in Spanish. "Ordered by Pez Espada and car-ried out by Estebán and Diego. I want Pez Espada. I want him for this."

"Before, when they roped us, when they poured kero-sene for the fire, you blamed me."

"As you say. I blamed you. How could I do other-wise? If you had not sided with the new American, the one who has replaced Huntington, foolishly because of the girl, because—"

"Shut up, shut your mouth!" Ruy cried, and ran, stag-gering, unsteady on his feet, for the car.

I got there a stride after he did and kept the door from shutting. He already had his hand on the ignition key. I struck it aside. He tried to fight me, and though I was weak and a little sick to my stomach from the smoke I'd inhaled, he was very much weaker. I pulled him from the car.

"We're all going," I said. "I'll do the driving. Do I have to rope you again?"

Ruy stared at the ground and didn't answer.

Paco said, "My little brother, he sits in front with you. I sit behind. He will remain docile, señor."

"That's fine. What about you?"

"I?"

"Last night Maruja told you to kill me. It wasn't your fault you didn't."

He laughed. I didn't laugh. He said, "Last night was last night. Tonight you have saved our lives. Tonight all I want is Pez Espada."

He was a thug and a highjacker and likely a killer, but he was a Spaniard with a Spaniard's code of honor. I believed him.

We piled in the way he had suggested. He sat on the edge of the rear seat, menacingly, behind his brother. Ruy stared at his lap. I started driving.

chapter twenty

I parked the Mercedes in a plaza two blocks up from the river gorge. Beyond the plaza the streets were too narrow, crooked and steep for the car. Twice, as we walked down one of them, our footsteps echoing on ancient cobblestones, a dark figure slipped out of a doorway, a furtive smalltime peddler offering us the detritus of the smugglers' trade.

"You wish fine Swiss watch, señores? Very good blocos, first-grade rubber of an incredible thinness? Cultured pearls from the Orient?"

They followed us a few paces and then drifted back into the shadows. We reached the bottom of the steep street. Crossing it like the bar of a T was a narrow street paralleling the river gorge.

"The third villa," Paco told me, pointing.

A row of what looked like one-story houses huddled

with their backs to the very edge of the chasm. Narrow paths roofed over with arbors separated them.

"There a back way in?" I asked.

"In back they are very big, these villas," Paco said. "Five and six stories and terraced gardens and steep stairs that go down and down until they reach the water."

"You armed?" I asked him.

He looked at me scathingly. "If I had a gun, you think Esteban and Diego would have left us to burn at the ranch? They were armed señor. Not us."

"Wait outside with your brother" I said. "Keep him quiet—even if you have to sit on him." Ruy had been broodingly silent on the drive back to Ronda. "I'm going in the back way. If anybody tries to leave the front, stop him. Okay?"

"Con mucho gusto," Paco said. His big, horse-like face smiled close to mine. "Police methods, eh, señor?" he said, enjoying himself. "I feel like a very agent of the Guardia."

I left them in front of the house. The windows in front were dark. The path along the side of the house smelled damply of exotic vegetation. Hanging vines brushed my face as I walked. Then I heard music—a sweet trumpet dominating a band in the swelling strains of *España Cani*. There was a large terrace in back, and big curtained French doors with light behind them. Small ornamental orange trees grew on the terrace. For no reason at all I went to the edge and looked over. There was another terrace below this one and a third below that—then blackness. A flight of stone stairs, almost as steep as an upright ladder, led down to the second terrace.

The Beretta felt light and serviceable in my hand. They had no reason to expect trouble, not here, not tonight. They'd paid off the cops, hadn't they?

Then, all of a sudden, I wasn't so sure. The fat colonel had broken up the possibility of a police raid, but instead of keeping me on ice until they cleared out of Ronda, he'd put me in the lockup only a few hours and then let me go. Why? Because there wasn't a hell of a lot a lone American could do? But why take chances?

Figure Pez Espada was calling the tune for the colonel. Did that mean he wanted me to drop in at the villa on the cliff—knowing what I'd find there and wanting me to find it? Or maybe it had been the colonel's idea. He could hold me but he couldn't kill me. Still, I knew too much, and Pez Espada wouldn't rest easy until I took what I knew to the grave with me. *Hold him, colonel. Hold the American, until we are ready. When we are ready, you will let him go, and he will come where, inevitably, he must come. And then we will kill him.* Like that?

I walked across the terrace to the French doors. The music had stopped. I heard footsteps, saw a woman's shadow move across the curtained glass of the doors. *España Cani* filled the night with sound again. The woman was playing a phonograph.

The door handle turned easily. The door swung in and the music was louder. I blinked at bright light, saw the five people seated in there and felt a little silly with the Beretta in my hand.

It was a large room, its stucco walls festooned with the impedimenta of bullfighting. There were gold and red formal capes, and small crimson killing capes, the muletas, stiff with bloodstains, and swords in their scabbards, and ribboned banderillas in clusters of four, and a picador's long stopped pick on hooks over the mantle and above that a stuffed and mounted bull's head. There were a few dozen photographs of toreros in their glittering finery, all of them smiling gravely, all of them autographed to Sr. Manzanarez who had taught them this and that and who had afición.

Of the five people sitting in that trophy room, none of them looking about to die of fright at my cloak-and-dagger entrance, only one was a man—and that one blind. The sculptor Fernando sat next to his North Country wife, who was telling him in low tones who had dropped in for a visit. Maruja, musky scent and all, stood near the phonograph. She turned the volume down and called me an unladylike name for what had happened last night, then turned the volume up, came over to me and said, "It is all over because you meddle, all over now and we must start as if from the beginning, elsewhere, because you meddle, and still you come here to meddle some more. What do you want here?"

"I get the idea," I said. "I'm a meddler. Go sit down somewhere."

"My boys will return soon," she crowed. "When they do, you will wish you hadn't meddled."

"I found your boys at Pez Espada's ranch. Roped to chairs with a fire burning all around them."

"What is this?" Her eyes widened with surprise and fear. "What is this you say?"

"Go let them in," I said. "They'll tell you."

She looked at me blankly.

"Front door," I said, and she went.

Nancy Huntington, stocky and not dressed in widow's weeds, was the fourth. She was wearing a strapless cotton dress and a mantilla on her hair and a single strand of pearls around her thick throat.

"What are you doing here?" I asked her.

But all she said was, "Oh, put that gun away, you horse's ass."

Tenley came over to me. She was number five. She tried to smile, and her ripe red lips trembled instead. "You said something about a fire, Chet. Is Ruy all right?"

I said that he was.

"Thank God."

North Country watched us. Nancy Huntington stared contemptuously at us. Tenley licked her lips, looked at me and then away. She was pale. "Did you come here looking for me?"

"And Pez Espada."

"He's gone. For good I think. And I'm perfectly safe. You shouldn't have bothered. You shouldn't—"

"Shouldn't have bothered?"

"I can take care of myself. Please, will you listen to me? Will you get out of here? Right now? That's all I ask." She came close to me and said very softly, "Remember how it could have been in Algeciras? I—I'll go with you if you want."

I thought she'd learned the truth about Ruy, that he was in as deep as his brother, as Pez Espada, and wanted to give him time to get away. The words came to my lips automatically, "Because of Ruy?"

Her tongue darted again, nervously. "Ruy? Yes, of course. Ruy. That's it. Did you save his life? I—I'm very grateful to you. I'm just asking you this one thing." I was looking down at those green eyes of hers over the high, wide-spaced cheekbones. She was gorgeous. "Please, Chet. Please go away." She sounded like a small child, intent and pleading: play the game the way I want and I'll be your best friend.

Nancy Huntington chortled in her whisky-voice, "Why don't you tell him about my lover, Tenley? Why don't you tell him that?" There was a bottle of Fundador on the table near where she sat. She poured and drank, and smirked at us. She was drunk, not drunk enough to fall off her chair, but too drunk to do anything but sit there heavy and flaccid while she said, "Why don't you tell the big detective man how come Stu was killed? Why don't you tell him how I was used? Used and abused by that horse's ass you call—"

Tenley, crossing the room swiftly to her, leaned down and slapped her face hard. The glass of Fundador flew. Amber liquid splashed in Nancy Huntington's eyes. Yelping, she knuckled them.

"Shut up, you're drunk," Tenley said. "Shut up." She turned to me. "What if I told you I had conclusive proof my father is dead? You came to Spain to find him, didn't you? So if he's dead .... will you go away, please?"

"If you don't tell him," Nancy Huntington threatened, "I will."

I stood there watching them. You walk into a movie theater in the middle of the picture, and the plot's involved and the actors say things at each other, simple words for their twelve-year-old audience, but with feeling, but until little fragments of what they say and do begin to form the logic of a story line, it's as if they're speaking a foreign language. I'd had that odd, disoriented feeling since entering Pez Espada's villa. The only thing that seemed to make sense was Tenley's assertion that her father was dead. It had seemed likely all along. But how had she found out?

"Let's hear it," I said.

"Hear it? Hear what?"

"Your father."

"This *I* have to hear," Nancy Huntington said. "This is going to be good."

Before Tenley could answer, Maruja, Paco and Ruy came in. They were walking side by side, woodenly.

Pez Espada, with a gun in his hand, walked behind them.

chapter twenty-one

"Put the gun down, Señor Drum," he said. "You cannot possibly shoot me without hurting one of them. I would have no difficulty shooting you."

I saw his face over Maruja's shoulder, just a face, any face in a crowd, except for the nose that had given him his name. But I saw the uncertainty in his eyes, the desperation, and the whiteness of his hand that clutched a short-barrel .32 revolver. He'd use the gun, all right. His left eyelid twitched. He'd use it for any reason or for no reason at all. What did he have to lose that he hadn't already lost? Besides, the fat colonel had set me free knowing I'd come here. If he was in deep enough with Pez Espada, he'd cover murder for him too.

I set the Beretta down on the phonograph cabinet. Reluctantly, but I did it. Pez Espada's interest swerved away from me. "Where is he?" he asked Tenley.

"Downstairs."

"Drinking?"

"Downstairs," Tenley said again.

Pez Espada shrugged. "I offered you all the chance to begin again," he said. "Here. Here in Spain, Alicante on the coast and the hills behind it. I have my contacts in Alicante. It could be the same as before. But no," he said, smiling bitterly, "you had to listen to a drunkard who—"

"I will work with you in Alicante," Fernando said.

"—could only think of fleeing, of leaving everything we had built together behind. Why? You great fools, didn't you know why? Because the building of it, the slow making of contacts, the artful smoothness of buying and then, instead of smuggling, highjacking our own cargoes—all that meant nothing to him. He hadn't seen it grow. He walked right into it, ready-made for him. When it began to crumble, why should he care? We have a fortune in contraband, he said. We can take it down to the coast, ship it to Morocco, he said, and everything we make will be profit. And you wanted to do it his way."

"Not I, señor," Fernando said. "Why do you think I

came here? When Maruja told me what he would charge for the diamonds—"

"The diamonds," said Pez Espada slowly, "are a sideline. Three, four times a year, and so easy to carry. We don't need a highjacking boat for the diamonds. No peasants and shopkeepers invest their pesetas in the diamonds. They are contraband before they even reach Gibraltar. The diamonds are carried as an accommodation to you. A man could bring the diamonds into Spain in his shoe. But the cigarettes, the automotive parts, the chapeaux from France, the medicines. . . . No, Fernando, I thank you; but you are not enough."

"Never have I tried to betray you," Fernando pleaded.

"No? Who was it who brought Huntington to the cave?"

Fernando blinked his blind eyes rapidly. "That? That was different. His wife told me Huntington had lost interest in the diamonds, saying they were too difficult to obtain in Gibraltar, saying there was too much danger. In the future he would concern himself with cigarettes, with automotive parts, with the other contraband you have mentioned. She said, if I went with Huntington to the cave, Maruja would convince him the diamonds were worthwhile."

"She lied to you," Pez Espada said flatly. "Huntington never intended to stop delivery of the diamonds. She is a whore and she had found a new lover and the new lover appealed to her as a man who could take her husband's place." Pez Espada jabbed his revolver into Maruja's back. "Which suited your schemes perfectly, eh gypsy woman? Eh?"

Maruja turned halfway around to face Pez Espada and his gun. That left his head exposed. The Beretta on the phonograph drew me. Snatch it up, pivot, fire in the same motion. . . .

And probably blow Maruja's head off. A revolver is not a rifle, and though I'm pretty good with one, nobody is that good.

"Huntington demanded too much," she said. "He did not have to face the risks we faced. He wanted more of the profits."

"Fool of a gypsy woman," said Pez Espada coldly, "we are not dealing in terms of a rucksack of contraband carried over the mountains and distributed by peddlers. We needed a man with contacts to dispose of large shipments. Huntington was that man."

"There was another."

"Huntington asked me for a bigger share. I agreed." Pez Espada shook his head. "It wasn't going to come out of *my* share."

"But ours?"

"Yours. Of course."

"The new one would have worked for less. He told Ruy that."

"Worked for less because he was worth less. You should have asked me. Huntington—he could snap his fingers and a wholesale distributor of cigarettes, complete with government license, would take ten thousand cartons in Malaga. Snap them again, and a garage in Valencia would buy a boatload of automotive parts. Snap them a third time, and a jeweler in Madrid—but what does it matter now? A wife who sleeps in any bed as long as there is a strange man in it, gypsy pack-rats too greedy to know a good thing when they see it, and Huntington is killed. Should I weep for you when Esteban and Diego are on their way to Alicante? Weep for those who deserted me when the new partner they thrust upon me decided to sell abroad?"

"There, you make a mistake," Maruja said. "I had made no decision as yet, señor. And when I make one, my boys obey."

Pez Espada laughed harshly. "Do they? They were going to drive the contraband from the ranch down to the coast at Marbella. They had friends there who could hide it until a boat could be found for the crossing to Africa. That was why Esteban and Diego did what they did."

"Ruy, he is young," Maruja said. "Blame Ruy, but it is nothing I cannot alter. He sees a skirt, he sees what is under that skirt, a foreign skirt, a clever and artful and evil woman, and the soft dark foreign trap there ensnares him and she leads him around as easily as one can goad an ox though she does it not for him but for—"

"Stop!" Ruy cried. "You can't talk about her like that. I love her."

Maruja recoiled from him as if she'd been struck physically by his words. "Love?" she said. "What do you know of love that I haven't taught you?"

Ruy took a deep breath. Very softly but distinctly he said, "What you taught me is filth. I know that now. It was you who could lead me around by a nose-ring. You— never anyone else. Did I ever see myself as a highjacker? As a criminal? Was it for that my father educated me? To be a man who could stand by while murder was done? But you and your black gypsy magic. . . . Tenley showed me what love could be like—clean and pure as the movement of a veronica." Comparing his relationship with Tenley with the art of a torero was the highest compliment he could pay.

Maruja called out, just his name, and on that one syllable her voice broke: "Ru-uy. . . ."

"You're filth," he said. "Even while my father still lived, even when I was a little boy, it is all I remember now of your love. How you took me to your bed, and first you sang to me, and then we played, and you gave me much wine to drink, and then more than played, and then with my father sick in the next room, we were like animals coupling, and that is what you call love."

Maruja screamed his name again, her voice breaking again, and clawed at his face with her hands. He struck her arms away contemptuously. Paco hit him, a single casual blow that sent him reeling across the room. He went down to his knees against the wall, stood up and grabbed a pair of barbed and ribboned banderillas off the wall.

Turning, raising the hooked sticks overhead, he strutted back across the room. He had everyone's attention, Pez Espada's included. I made a grab for the Beretta. Then Ruy leaped across my line of vision, making straight for his brother and Maruja with the bright banderillas. At the last instant he swerved, as if the bull, too, that only he could see had swerved. "Here, toro; hey, toro!" he cried, and I had time to realize Paco wasn't the only one Pez Espada had slated for death in the burning ranch, and Pez Espada had time to fire—once, the small revolver making a flat, cracking sound, the slug taking Ruy in the chest and halting him momentarily before he stood high on his toes like a ballet dancer and drove the sharp hooked barbs of the banderillas, one on either side, into the soft meatiness of Pez Espada where shoulders and throat met, drove them in deeply and then collapsed on the floor.

Pez Espada dropped the revolver. He grasped the hafts of the banderillas and pulled. The barbs wouldn't come free. There was very little blood at first, but his face had drained white. He shook himself the way a bull that has just received the banderillas shakes itself, and the sticks rattled. Then he grasped them again, his eyes wild, and tugged as hard as he could. The hook between his left shoulder and throat found the carotid artery. Dark blood swelled, pumped, jetted—and still Pez Espada pulled and twisted the banderilla.

He fell near Ruy, his hands still on the brightly-colored stick. Tenley whimpered. I reached Ruy before she did, and felt for his pulse. I shook my head. It was not necessary to feel for Pez Espada's pulse. He had lost too much blood.

Then Tenley turned away and whimpered again, and I saw a man, big and in a rumpled, white linen suit, handsome but needing a haircut as he had needed a haircut on the picture his father had shown me in the States, standing in front of the French doors.

I should have been surprised. An hour ago I would have been. I wasn't now. There was, of course, only one man he could be.

Robbie Hartshorn.

chapter twenty-two

He swayed there before the doors that led out to the terrace. I remembered what Tenley had said at the very beginning. He was drunk. He stayed drunk from the time he woke up until he brushed his teeth with bonded bourbon at night.

Despite the lines and wrinkles of dissipation, despite the dark, swollen smudges under his eyes, his face had an unformed look—not vacuous but blank like the face of a very young man still unscarred by life and the difficult job of survival in a world none of us ever makes.

"You had proof, you had incontrovertible proof," Nancy Huntington told Tenley mockingly, "that your father was dead."

Tenley looked at me. She had no words, but her eyes

said it: what else could I have done? What else could I do? *I guess pity is the worst emotion you can feel for someone you love, but that's the way I feel.*

Tenley went to him. Ruy was dead. Ruy wouldn't need her now. "Dad, this man was sent from the States to ... find you."

"The Governor sent him?"

"Yes, Dad. The Governor."

"Congratulations," said Robbie Hartshorn, smiling at me. "It would seem you've found me. That's more than I've ever been able to do, and I've been looking for years. When you fly back you can tell the Governor when last seen I was heading for Africa with a fortune in contraband. I won't need him any more. I won't need the monthly check. I won't need the sanctimonious sermons that come with it."

"Dad," Tenley said, "get a grip on yourself, please. That's not the way it's going to be. They're on their way to Alicante. Diego and Estebán. With the contraband."

He said, "That's ridiculous. You don't know what you're talking about. Paco and Ruy—"

"Ruy is dead."

He saw Ruy and Pez Espada on the floor then. He went slowly to them, fifteen years of heavy drinking and fifteen years of experience with too much alcohol making it possible for him to do it without staggering. He bent near Ruy, clucking his tongue. Maruja was already there, her head on the boy's chest, crying. Paco was squatting near her, trying to comfort the gypsy woman with clumsy words and the gentle touch of a huge hand. Robbie Hartshorn bent again near Pez Espada. He stood and turned slowly.

"I'm going to Africa," he said. "You see, I'm going after all." He was holding Pez Espada's gun.

"You're not going anywhere," I said. "You're too drunk to shoot straight. I'm not."

"But I'm desperate, mister. I'm desperate, and you're not."

We stood facing each other. He glanced down at the gun in his hand, as if surprised to see it. I could have shot him then. I didn't. He wasn't ready to fire, just as I hadn't been sent to Spain to kill him.

"I'm going to Africa," he said again, as if trying to convince himself.

"What will it get you?" I said. "A couple of weeks of running? You won't get far."

"That's the story of my life, old man. I never got very far."

I took a slow step toward him and said, "You got sick and tired of the Governor's checks and sermons, so you had to go out and earn a pile for yourself—the hard way."

"Every month," he said. He mimed the Governor's voice: " 'My dear boy, don't you think it's time you settled down to some valuable work, valuable at least to you if not to the community?' I almost puked every time I opened his monthly letter. I couldn't stand it any longer. I just couldn't."

I took another step. If he noticed it, it meant nothing to him. The gun was held slackly in his hand. "So you decided to try your hand with the highjackers?"

"Of course, old man. Stu Huntington was a drunk, you know. Aren't we all, all honorable drunks? The soused society of remittance men. He'd talk a little every now and then until I had the whole picture. How they operated. Pez Espada as broker for the cargoes, the Fuentes brothers highjacking with the Jímenez boat, Stu disposing of the contraband. I found his list of contacts, and the rest just sort of fell into place."

"There were two people you had to work on," I said, and by then I'd cut the distance between us in half. "The first was Nancy Huntington. The second——"

"Ah yes," he said, "the fat, frowsy Nancy. Actually, I didn't 'find' her husband's list. She gave it to me. She detested him, you see. Or so she said. I suppose she really did, and if so, he was the only male of the species she ever detested. It was easy to convince her we could run off together with a few hundred thousand dollars worth of contraband. Not that I would have taken her with me, old man. But she leaped at the chance."

"The Fuentes brothers and Maruja were disturbed because Huntington was upping his own take at their expense—which gave you the opportunity you needed."

"Pero cómo no?" he said in Spanish. "But why not? Ruy was easy to work on, figuring if we were working together I couldn't very well disapprove of his relationship with Tenley. But of course I had no intention of working with them, not permanently. I just wanted to make my pile, old man, and then be free of them. Of all of them. The Governor and his checks and sermons, my wife and the way one minute she wanted to possess me utterly, telling me what a perfect marriage we had and no one understood us and we were so wonderful together, the next minute going off solitary as a cat. . . . It got so I couldn't stand it. If I had money, if I were of independent means. . . . "

"You told Ruy you could do everything Huntington did, and for less money. He told Maruja and Paco, and Nancy Huntington arranged for Fernando to drive with her husband to the cave in Fuengirola. Where they killed him."

"Not Ruy," Robbie Hartshorn said. "Paco did it, hitting him with a tire-iron. Then, once it was done, of course, Ruy couldn't very well turn his family in."

"That was when I came along," I said. "Paco and Ruy already were scared because I was looking for you, and then when I showed up at the cave the night Huntington was murdered, they decided to make it a doubleheader. It would be made to look like an accident, and Sergeant Martinez, being on the take, would close his books on it as an accident. The only trouble was, I got out alive."

"Ruy had nothing to do with that either," Robbie Hartshorn said slowly. Though he was looking at me, his words were for Tenley. "I'd have no reason to say this, old man, no reason at all because the boy is dead, unless it were the truth. Ruy was confused, and the gypsy could wrap him around her little finger, but he was no killer. He never was a killer. You must understand that. He never was a killer."

"Then," I went on, and by then I was very close to him, "Martinez dutifully tried to scare me off by saying I'd been seen—indicating that he meant in a compromising position—with Nancy Huntington. If it was murder, I would be a likely suspect. So I was supposed to lope off for the nearest airport with my tail between my legs. And that idea was put in his head by the one person who could have put it there, the only one who saw us on the terrace of La Atalaya the night before the murder, the only one who could claim we did anything but say a few words—Nancy Huntington herself."

I was almost close enough to take the gun from his hand. I said, "Martinez let me go that time, but then after I'd been to Algeciras to see Pez Espada he set me up with a pro in a Fuengirola hotel, and that's when I got the boot. But he never would have condoned highjacking; smuggling, that was something else. I put a bug in his ear, and he did some investigating, and that's when the roof started to fall in. Rafael Jímenez in Carihuela, a man named Short in Torremolinos, Pez Espada in Algeciras—"

"Swordfish came here. We could start again in Alicante, he said, and probably he was right. But I'd never wanted that, not in Fuengirola and not in Alicante either. I said Africa, and Ruy backed me because after all I was Tenley's father, and I still don't know why it didn't work out that way."

"Estebán and Diego were just a little bit tougher than Ruy and Paco," I told him.

Then suddenly he smiled and thrust the gun in my hand and said, "Will you kindly stop sneaking up on me like an elephant trying to walk on tiptoe, old man? Here—is this what you want?"

That gave me a gun in each hand. Robbie Hartshorn looked at them and at me, and briefly and with regret at Tenley. Then he turned and walked out through the French doors. I went after him, fast. Just as he hadn't taken a shot at me, I didn't fire at him. I couldn't shoot him in the back. A gun wasn't the final answer. Except in the black and white world of TV, it never is.

He was running, and he didn't have far to go. He climbed the low terrace wall and sat there. "Keep back," he warned me. I couldn't see his face in the darkness.

"I want Tenley to think the boy was better than he was," he said in a conversational tone. "That's very important, old man. And I want her to think I—I couldn't shoot you. I couldn't, you know. Not in front of her."

Tenley came out. I turned at the sound of her footsteps. She screamed. When I pivoted again, the terrace was empty.

Robbie Hartshorn had a long way to fall.

chapter twenty-three

Paco made a run for it while we were on the terrace. I caught him at the door and fired once over his head. He came back inside with his hands up.

After that, I picked up the phone and called the Guardia. The fat colonel and a platoon of winged patent-leather hats arrived in less than ten minutes. With Pez Espada dead, the colonel was all through covering up. He fell on Paco and Maruja like a ton of bricks. The charge was murder, and Nancy Huntington and Fernando would be booked, he said, as the Spanish equivalent of accessories before the fact.

Nancy Huntington called us all horse's asses. "How could I help murder my own husband?" she wailed.

North Country told her: "For you, love, it was easy."

The colonel was all politeness and sympathy to Tenley. He put her up in the Victoria hotel. She was questioned there, gently and with restraint. The colonel was a true Spanish gentleman—once the hand that fed him was cut off at the wrist.

I had the room next to Tenley's at the Victoria. By two in the morning the Guardia were through with us, and I turned in. I heard Tenley's door open and shut before I'd taken my shoes off. I followed her along the deserted corridor.

She went outside, and down through the Victoria's gardens and along the path that led to the paseo, a park on the edge of Ronda's high cliff. She sat on the rampart there with a million stars over her head.

"You must be all in," I said softly.

"No, it's funny, but I'm not sleepy." She stared down eight hundred feet to the blackness that was the valley of the Serena. "He took me here when I was a little girl," she said. "He wasn't drinking so much then. An old Spanish teller of tall tales came over and fed us a yarn. I'd been throwing St. John's breads over and watching how the up-drafts brought them back. He saw a man throw a dog over, the old man told us. Two hours later the dog reappeared, on the very same spot."

She kept on staring. She was silent.

"What are you going to do?"

"I've got to stay with Mother now. She'll need me. But not here. I'm taking her back to the States. You think she'll come?"

"If you work on her, she'll come."

"Was my father a killer?" Tenley asked suddenly.

I said nothing.

"It was his idea to kill Huntington, wasn't it?"

"He just wanted to ease Huntington out of the picture," I said, remembering the man sitting on the terrace wall as Tenley was sitting on the rampart of the paseo. "Paco killed him."

"But my father—"

"Listen," I said. "He could have shot me tonight. He didn't."

"You were armed too."

"He couldn't do it," I said. "He couldn't kill a man in cold blood—any more than Ruy could have."

"You really think so?"

I looked at her back. "I'm sure of it," I said.

She sighed, and then she started to cry. I led her back inside, and this time she slept like a baby.

They wanted to hold us in Torremolinos until the trial, but the Governor pulled the strings that a Governor could pull, and they were satisfied with our signed depositions instead.

Three days after we returned to the coast, we took off from Malaga on the first leg of our flight home. Andrea Hartshorn wasn't drinking. She had found strength in Tenley, and with all the weight of her grief was leaning on it. I thought it would do Tenley more good than it did her.

The last I heard, the Guardia were looking for Esteban and Diego—without any success and not very hard.

THE END

www.ingramcontent.com/pod-product-compliance
Lightning Source LLC
Chambersburg PA
CBHW030618130626
46552CB00002B/628